SAFE INSIDE
THE VIOLENCE

CHRISTOPHER IRVIN

SAFE INSIDE THE VIOLENCE

CRIME STORIES

Jan!
Always great to see you. Hope
you enjoy!

280 STEPS

NECON 36

A 280 Steps Original

This is a work of fiction. Names, characters, places, and incidents are either the product of the author's imagination or are used fictitiously. Any resemblance to actual events or locales or persons, living or dead, is entirely coincidental.

ISBN 978-82-93326-70-0

Cover design by Risa Rodil

To Jenni

Contents

Union Man

LEM took his time approaching the mob in front of the steel mill, taking deep breaths, trying to rub out the knot in his stomach. His pocket like a cheek packed full of tobacco, stretching with each step. As he cleared the crest of the last hill, he paused. For the first time in memory the sky was clear of black smoke. He could see the deep navy swirls of the Ohio River, and rich yellows and greens of the farmland that surrounded Pittsburgh. He wished his son could be standing there with him, looking down upon the forgotten beauty of their city. His gaze turned to the space beside him, to where he'd be holding Henry's hand as he told him, *this was how it used to be*. He swore before it was all over he'd bring him to that very spot, carry him if need be.

A chant for more pay and improved working conditions rose from the picket line, a reminder of the chaos that had shut down the smoke stacks. It was the tenth day of the strike. The tenth day of the throng of work replaced by the shouts of men. The tenth day without pay.

A twinge of pain arc up his leg as he stepped to avoid a dip in the road, thick with mud from the previous night's rain. When sides failed to reach an agreement on a new contract, the Baron ordered the mill closed, locking the workers out. Those protesting on the inside were assaulted by security. Lem suffered a busted ankle during the brief scuffle. The injury had sent him home but it wasn't what kept him there.

"You're late for your shift." The union boss sat comfortable on a stack of wooden crates, directing strikers from afar. He tossed the charred remains of a cigarette to the ground and spit. "Lots changed since you was here."

Lem looked past the growing mob and into the mill. Ugly barbed wire had been strung through the perimeter fence and two men stood with water cannons atop towering platforms on either side of the main gate.

"It's gettin' serious now, Lem." The man chuckled after the comment, as if ten days without pay wasn't serious enough. Lem kept his mouth shut, gritting his teeth to keep the uneasiness from flaring up again. He'd already vomited once on the way in. Didn't have much left.

"Grab one of the signs from Tommy over there and get in line." Lem nodded and continued his slow pace, his feet heavy. The sound of the river increased to a dull roar, adding an undercurrent to the strikers' furor.

"Hey, Lem!" A shout from behind—the union boss. "Goldman pay you a visit?"

Lem's back broke out in a sweat. Almost kept walking, but thought better of it. "Yessir, he did."

"And how's your son?" He said, again, with the same uncomfortable smile.

"Better." It was a lie so hard he had to turn back before

the man could read it on his face.

***

Lem had not been expecting visitors when Goldman rapped on his front door. The soft tapping of his knuckles like a wind-blown tree branch on the side of the apartment. Lem approached the door cautiously, opening it a crack until he could take in the full length of the man. Then, perplexed, pulled the door wide. Lem had never met such a well-dressed individual in his life. The union man wore a gray three piece suit, complete with maroon tie and matching kerchief. When Goldman removed his top hat, introduced himself and asked to come inside, Lem fixated on the gold chain of a pocket watch hung from his breast pocket. Lem glanced around, embarrassed at the unfit conditions of the apartment for a man like Goldman to be visiting.

Goldman waved his hand, as if trying to dismiss Lem's anxiety. "I'm here to see you," he said. The gesture did little to calm his nerves. He was a regular at the mill, no different than any other.

"I'm told you were there when the fighting broke out. Heard you took a bit of a tumble."

"Yessir, I was. The ankle's much better, thank you." He felt ashamed to address the injury, like a helpless boy who couldn't defend himself from a bully. The swelling around the joint had dispersed but deep purple bruising remained. A *real man* would have sucked it up and stuck to the picket line. A martyr for the cause. He'd been reminded of this before and expected to hear it again.

"I know the ankle is better. You think we'd let you stay out on a bum leg?"

Lem eyed the floor. He couldn't afford to lose his job at the mill.

"I'm here about your son. How is he?"

The question made Lem pause. There was a level of sincerity in Goldman's voice that had been missing before. "The doc says it's influenza. He's strong but—"

"But nothing." He put a palm on Lem's shoulder. "May I see the boy?"

Lem led Goldman through the tiny house to Henry's room. His wife sat asleep in the nearby rocking chair, exhausted from the overnight watch. Goldman crossed the space to the bed in one long stride, stepping softly to lessen the creak of the floorboards. He stood next to Henry, running his fingers around the rim of his hat as he eyed the pale clammy flesh, like he was paying his final respects at a funeral. Lem stood in the doorway admiring his wife's courage. She'd done so well, stayed so positive through the week. Goldman returned to Lem, guiding him out of the room and into the hallway. They spoke in whispers.

"I know a physician in town from Chicago who may be of some assistance. Unfortunately, he is tied to the mill for the duration of the strike, and there's no telling how long it could last. We need to get the public fully on our side to end this stalemate. Do you understand me, Lem? Their support is vital to our cause."

Lem felt the knot in his stomach twist.

"Now listen. The Baron has continued to add security but with little confrontation."

"We was told no weapons by the strike leaders. That it's to be a peaceful strike," Lem said, regurgitating drilled commandments as best he could.

"Yes, and they are doing an excellent job of keeping the men in line. Unfortunately too good a job."

Lem swallowed down the sickness in his throat. He knew where this was going.

"The people of Pittsburgh want action. The press wants blood." He put his hands on Lem's shoulders and lowered himself to see eye to eye. "Can I count on you when the time comes to do the right thing?"

Lem gave a slight nod, a biological response to a question his brain could barely begin to process. Goldman donned his hat and turned to leave. He sealed the deal with one foot out the door.

"Lem," he said. "Think of your son."

***

Tommy pulled Lem close in a swift hug, greeting him amongst the gallery of signs pasted with blood-red paint. They'd grown up together in the countryside, taken jobs at the mill around the same time. Tommy was one of the few in the union he'd call a close friend.

"How is Henry, truly now?"

Lem took a deep breath. Wiped his palms on his shirt, feeling the dampness of his son's bed sheets, the fever on his forehead. He couldn't open his mouth to spill the words, bring truth to his hopeless thoughts. Tommy's shoulders drooped. "Go home, Lem. We got more than enough here to man the strike."

Lem pinched the bridge of his nose, closed his eyes tight. A tear squeezed out onto his cheek and he wiped it away. "No, my place is here. They're sending a doctor, a man from Chicago."

"Well, that's mighty nice of them." He clasped Lem's arm. "Good to see those union boys at the top takin' care of their own." He turned back to his collection and fished for the proper sign. "We'll get through this together." He found what he was looking for, along with a section of rope.

"Quite the lump you've got on that leg of yours." Lem covered it with his hand when Tommy looked like he meant to reach out and touch it. "Don't want to end up on the bottom like last time?"

Tommy whispered as he hung the sign around Lem's neck. "Be careful where ya flash that, tempers been flarin' since you was here." He took a step back to admire his work. The small sign read STRIKE, brushed on with a rough hand. "That'll do. At least it won't weigh ya down."

The rough cord strung through the wood chaffed against Lem's neck. The day had turned hot and he wished he had worn a hat, something to keep part of him in the shade, hidden from the sun that seemed to follow him like a spotlight in a dark theater. He hadn't felt such a nervous twitch in his heart since he was seven years old, walking into church, mouth and pockets stuffed with stolen licorice candy. No one knew, and yet everyone knew. It had been written then, as it was now, on his burning cheeks. Like all men, Lem grew to learn to hide his intentions, but some things are just too big to keep from bubbling to the surface.

Familiar and unfamiliar faces alike greeted him as he pressed himself into the crowd. The noon shift change at the picketing line meant most, if not all, of the hundreds of steel workers were present around the mill. Lem could feel the stress emanating from the men, but the strike bosses in front still commanded respect. If you didn't count the bar fights in town, the aggression had been kept in check since they were forced out of the compound. It made sense. Besides the few guards on the other side of the fence, the only ones they had to pick fights with were themselves.

"Pinks!"

The shout came from the direction of the riverbank. A group of workers surrounding Lem pushed their way across the mob, taking Lem with them, swept up in the sudden fervor. His secret threatened to pop out, but quick-like he caught it and thrust it back in, keeping a thumb across his pant leg to get a better grip. A small army of tailored suits and polished shoes approached the riverbank on board a barge built for hauling metal. One hundred? Two hundred? Lem quickly lost count as the Pinkertons unslung their rifles and prepared to come ashore.

The group chant reduced to a murmur as strikers eyed each other, their leaders for direction. What now? The Pinkertons wore their brutal reputation on their smug faces like all the stories and rumors were true. Men and women beaten to death in front of their families. Union bosses tortured into folding their cards. They didn't call them 'strike-breakers' for nothing. Lem swallowed hard and reached into his pocket.

He gripped the sweat-polished stone loosely in the palm of his left hand. Round like a baseball. He'd woken early and spent the morning pacing the fields alongside the gravel road that lead to the mill on the outskirts of the city. After much tribulation he settled on a black rock with swirls of gray and speckled like the night stars. It stood out among the jagged, reddish-clay colored stones, like the one he'd been pelted with as a kid by a bully looking for trouble. The rock had hit him square in the face with a sharp edge that slashed his cheek, made him bleed and gave him a permanent scar—a thin line below his eye when he smiled. So he spent the better part of the morning rolling the stone in his hand, hoping somehow his sweat would tumble any edges, like a river might grind its keep.

"Look at them Pinks, just waitin' for a reason to come at us," a voice, somewhere behind Lem said.

Lem tugged at the rope around his neck, his nerves reaching toward a crescendo he couldn't possibly hope to contain. A terrible itch grew upward from his toes, like he'd stepped on an ant hill and the tiny insects sought immediate revenge. He licked his cracked lips, a sudden dizziness tugging his soul skyward.

And then, squeezing the stone so hard his tendons threatened to snap, the feelings vanished, replaced by a great emptiness at the sight of the couple beside him. The evening shift leader, his shirt soaked through with sweat, firm grip on his son's shoulder. The boy, dressed fit for Sunday church, couldn't be much older than ten. He stood tall, slightly wavering as if he might catch a narrow window between the backs of the men in front.

Think of your son.

Lem wiped the mistiness from his eyes, unsure if the despair worming through his veins was for the boy, or himself, and the nightmare of this terrible day he knew would haunt him if he let the stone fly. The sudden uncertainty struck Lem in the gut. Would the doctor leave this boy to see to his own? What of the other injured?

"I shouldn't be here... I should be with Henry," he said to himself.

Before Lem could push his way out of the crowd, a shoulder crashed into his back and the stone slipped from his hand, slapping the muck at his feet. He froze, eyes locked on the horizon.

"First day back and itchin' for a little trouble, eh Lem?" Fitz clapped him hard around the collar, gave a him a shake. Built like an ox, Fitz handled Lem like his insides were stuffed with cotton. Fitz bent down, retrieved the stone and after giving it a good review, stuffed it into Lem's hand. "Didn't pick you as the type. Figured you was a union man through and through."

Lem rubbed his sore neck, stared hard at Fitz. The man was a constant pain, his machismo on full display. "No need to get defensive now. You think you were the only one?" Lem continued in hot silence, his face flaring ruby red. "What'd he get you for? A couple loaves of bread?" Fitz snickered. "You married men are too easy. Whatever the bitch wants, am I right?" He laughed again, this time turning heads, interested in the commotion. Lem's knuckles whitened around the stone. "Hope it was worth it. Me? I just do it for the fun." Fitz lifted his shirt and exposed the pistol. "Let's give these Pinkerton sons of bitches what they came for."

Then the pistol was out, a glistening finger wrapped around the trigger. Lem swung in a wide arc, his muscles reacting in shock before his brain could catch the signals. The stone cuffed Fitz in the back of the head, felling the man's aim as he squeezed the trigger, shooting a fellow striker in the back. Lem grabbed for the gun, fingers fumbling with nervous energy, but Fitz recovered and was too strong, roaring with anger as he knocked Lem back into the crowd.

Again, he took aim, this time the bullet sailing through and into the militia. A man's gargled scream was silenced by the boom of return fire. Fitz dropped the weapon, ducked and bolted through the crowd, his size easily bowling over those in his path. It all happened so fast, and yet when the concussion from first shot rippled through Lem's ear drums, time slowed to a crawl. All he could hear was the sound of his lungs as he gasped for air, pushing down the shock of the gunfire.

Think of your son.

Lem let the stone fall to the mud, felt a cool breeze lick his sticky fingers, tickle even, like he'd run his hand through his son's wispy hair. Then something sharp, like a bee sting slapped his hand back hard. The man in front of him jolted backwards onto Lem, going limp. Lem felt his ankle buckle and then they were falling together, down under the mob. He struggled in the mud, his arms flailing for something to grip onto and pull himself up. The mob erupted into a full stampede, strikers sprinting in every direction, tripping over Lem and the body that lay on top of his legs. Lem pushed himself up to a sitting position, grunting through screams of the injured.

Think of your son.

He cried out, his ankle howling in response to his attempt to twist his leg. Then his vision exploded with a swarm of fireflies as a knee caught him in the back of the head. He wavered upright for a moment, looping his fingers through the dying man's suspenders to save himself from being trampled as all dimmed and then went black.

He awoke in a chair that creaked in tune with the floor as he rocked back and forth. The room smelled of lye soap with a hint of dirt that had been washed away. The brightness was too much for his eyes and when he rubbed them he found his left hand wrapped in bandages, pointer and middle fingers gone. If he squinted hard enough he could see their ghosts wiggle.

"Momma?" The little voice echoed in his head. Or was it in the house?

"Henry?" He looked past his hand, felt his heart collapse. His son's bed had been stripped bare.

Footsteps, he swore he heard them. "Henry!" His voice had gone hoarse, barely louder than a whisper. He tried to stand, but the pain in his ankle dropped him to the floor. The strike, the stone, the chaos, everything spinning back to him. He held on tight to the bed as the painful memories hit him in waves, the dark threatening to drown him.

"Dad?" Lem saw only a shadow at first, black with a silver outline.

"Dad?" Henry's voice echoed again. Lem gripped

the mattress so tight his hand began to bleed. His heart boomed like the flat-footed stomps of his son's feet, as loud as gunshots.

Outside, a light wind rustled the trees, dissolving the black shadow in the hallway. Lem cocked his head to listen, but heard nothing over the anguish of his own voice as he wept, alone in an empty house.

Imaginary Drugs

DONNY cuts the tip off a plastic Pixy Stix with a switchblade he keeps in the back pocket of his swim trunks. Part of me thinks it must be uncomfortable to sit in the lifeguard stand for long stretches of time with a piece of metal wedged beneath you, but I don't say anything. Next summer I'll have one too.

"Practice," he says, dumping half the orange contents onto a bench that I'd wiped down with a bleach-soaked rag moments before. "This will get you ready for the good stuff."

The damp cement floor is cold, the morning sun teasing through narrow slits that top the walls of the boys' locker room. Donny sits further down the bench, a smile on his face the whole time. His tan, chiseled frame is mostly hidden in shadow except for his straight teeth and naturally bleached hair. At sixteen, he's a year older and everything I want to be. I'm on my knees, nose hovering over the powder, eager to please. What can I say? Mom tells me I'm an impressionable kid. That's part of why I'm here, to get away from the city.

I press an index finger over my left nostril like Tony

Montana and snort a face full of sugar. For a split second it burns like a lit match has been shoved up my nose, then it's all orange down the back of my throat. I hold back a cough until I have to swallow. It takes a minute for me to get it under control because I'm busy trying to force the rest down, to look like I can handle it. Tough it out like camp counselors instruct kids with bee stings and poison ivy and tears in their eyes to do. When I finally glance up the smile is gone. He looks bored.

Outside, a bell rings signaling the opening of the pool. Donny pulls sunglasses down over his eyes and stands to leave. He's first shift. On the way out he tosses the Stix in the trash and tells me to clean myself up. I hurry to follow, brushing the rest of the powder onto the tile floor. Most ends up on my palms, orange streaks against my navy blue swim trunks before I can think, focused on chasing the thwack-thwack of Donny's sandals.

I catch up to him in the hallway that leads outside to the pool. Kids are laughing in the distance, coming through the gates. The water won't be warm for another hour, maybe two if the clouds stick around.

"Donny." I grab for his arm. "When—" It's all I get out before he spins, lowering his shoulder and slamming me into the cinderblock wall. Tiny stars wink in and out, circling Donny's ruffled hair like a crown. He says something about me not paying attention and pulls my lanyard tight around my throat. A summer's worth of heat emanates from his skin. His breath smells of orange, and I wonder if he finished off the Stix before he threw it out, or if my sense of smell is permanently damaged. I focus on the bewildered face reflected in his shades.

The rest of the day will be spent on eggshells.

I stay behind, count to thirty in my head to give Donny some room. He doesn't want to be seen leaving the locker room with me. It's okay, not everyone can come tonight. I wade through the crush of campers, shouting and chasing each other inside to claim the same areas they've claimed all summer. I shout at them to walk but none of them notice.

A fat kid sporting a thick mop of hair hip-checks his counterpart, still fully dressed, jean shorts and all, into the deep end. He swings his backpack off his shoulder mid-flight before everything he owns gets soaked. It lands with a dull thud in the gutter, safe until his splash sends a wave that soaks the bottom. Donny blows his whistle, adjusts his posture to make it look like he's coming down and commands the clowns to cut it out. Half the kids in the vicinity turn to look up at him, wonder if what they're doing is wrong. The dry one lowers his head in shame, mutters sorry and bends to lend a hand, only to be pulled in as well. Then they're both laughing, darting around with surprising speed, like two whales that'd spent their lives lost, uncomfortable on the surface. It all makes me angry in a way I don't understand.

I leave them and shuffle around the deck to an area marked off by lane lines for lap swimmers. The old guy who runs the place swims laps at night. He wears black goggles, a clip over his nose, and a speedo because it helps cut the draft. That's what he told me anyway, like he needed an excuse. There was a schedule to work nights, but that ended after the first week. I heard a rumor that parents complained because we weren't being paid for it. There were others too, but that's what we settled on.

I kneel beside the gutter, dip my hands into the chlorinated water and rub them together. The bottom of the pool is bright white, making tiny piles of sand and grit visible even in the deepest end where the signs state it's safe to dive. I shake off the excess and dry my palms against my thighs, erasing the last of the evidence on my suit. When I look up one of Donny's boys has a smirk on his face like he's in on it all. I pull my sunglasses over my eyes, disguising the fact that I'm still watching him, wondering what Donny sees in the asshole.

There are six stands for the eight lifeguards on duty. Machiko and I are the least senior of the group, but bathroom duty grants us an extra thirty minutes to relax before entering the rotation. Machiko's hunched over a chair on the far side of the pool deck, towel in hand, face hidden beneath her hood. Each morning she circles the deck, meticulously wiping dew from chairs that kids will splash on throughout the day. The repetition puts her in a meditative state. She tried explaining it once, how calm it makes her feel. I don't have the patience; besides, she wouldn't let me try anyway. *This not karate kid*, she'd said, faking the accent everyone assumes she has before she can even open her mouth. We both laughed, but I could tell deep down she was serious. I sit down next to her on one she's just finished, and she eyes my damp suit like I'm encroaching on her ritual.

"I'm dry." I hold my hands up, innocent. "I swear."

"Not what it looks like."

"Mostly, then. I don't have a towel." A group of kids toss their bags on a set of chairs Machiko has yet to reach.

She's behind today. It disgusts her.

"Here," she says, tossing her damp rag over my head. "I give up."

"Gross." I crumple it into a ball and stuff it beneath the chair. It reeks of dirt and mildew. "What did you think of the end? You finished, right?"

Machiko pulls the back of her chair up and lays down, chin up toward the clouds, eyes on where the sun ought to be, like she's about to confess a secret, or fall asleep.

"I told you, I don't like robots."

"How can you not like robots?" I lean back, feel my cheeks growing hot. All summer we've spent our breaks reading manga—his and hers kind of stuff—until someone swiped her collection last week from her room. Counselors took down the incident with little fanfare. No one was questioned, all focused on collecting their last paychecks and going home. I surprised her the night after the theft, dropping off my books to cheer her up. She invited me in, tears welling in her eyes as she turned the pages. Whatever we'd been missing that felt real that night, is gone now. Our friendship tinged with fraud.

"All they do is shoot their lasers back and forth at each other." She forms a pistol with her right hand, slaps at the trigger with her index finger. "Faceless, expendable men going boom. Why?"

"To protect Earth?" I say. I've read all twenty volumes cover to cover twice and she still makes me question myself. The excitement of the moment is dwindling. I regret ever sharing. She'll be there, poking around inside my head if I ever open one of them again.

"They're in space," she says. "There should be enough

room up there for them all to fly around without blowing each other up. It's infinite."

"All they do in your books is go to school and gossip."

"That's life."

"That's boring."

A grin spreads across her face at my frustration, like she's won a game I didn't know we were playing. The conversation drifts off. Kids drop cannonballs and can openers that splash our legs. Last days are hard, more time spent on how to say goodbye than actually saying it. My stomach turns with bittersweet anxiety.

"Going out with Donny tonight? To the overlook?" she says, turning her head toward me, reading my reaction. Her tone is serious. I can't tell if it's a statement or a question. I glimpse Donny out of the corner of my vision. He gives me a nod, a slight dip of his chin. It barely registers—it's only meant for me—but it carries like a fist bump or a high five. We're cool. I got this. But still I can't bear to look at her.

"What are you talking about?" The lie is so blatant I even chuckle. Her eyes don't leave me alone until I meet them.

"Need a date?"

"After all this?" I gesture to the sky, like there really are invisible armies of robots clashing in the far reaches of space.

"Anything to save me from counselor karaoke, or whatever they have planned for tonight's assembly. I'm already packed. Tomorrow can't come soon enough."

"It's kind of an invite-only thing."

"One of those, huh?"

"What's that supposed to mean?"

She shrugs, her attention back on the kids. Donny chirps his whistle, signaling the shift change. "You're better than those guys sitting up there."

"Yeah, yeah. Tell it to the robots."

I head for the stand that looks over the shallows and enter the rotation. The other lifeguards take their time climbing down, transitioning to their next post.

Donny's last. He swings from the chair to the deck, skipping the ladder, taking the six foot drop with ease. He passes Machiko on the way to the snack shack. Except for his laughter, I'm too far away to hear what he says to her. She ignores him, wraps her arms around her legs and pulls them in close for warmth.

She spends most of her days at the pool in sweats, even when the sun hangs blistering overhead. Says she gets cold easily up in the chair. The breeze over her exposed toes reverberates up her entire body. She worries about what will happen if she has to jump in to rescue one of the campers. When her body splashes down in the cold water, will she freeze and sink to the bottom, muscles locked in place, eyes unable to leave those of the child she was supposed to save? I told her I don't know, that I've never known anyone in need of saving. I secretly hope I never do.

Becky did though, shattering her knee cap jumping into the shallows to save a three year old who'd walked straight into the pool from the graduated end. Right up until his head went under. She got him out, but it ended her summer. Prior to the injury, she would boast about how fast she'd been able to rescue kids, how many kids' lives she'd saved. When she dropped in on crutches to say goodbye, it became a highlight reel of how she'd sacrificed for the cause. Machiko thought it was the pain medication speaking. I think it's what she wanted all along.

My shift continues uneventfully, which is good because half my brain is focused on tonight. I'm one of five he's invited—that's all that will fit in the beat-up sedan he bought with last summer's pay. At sunset we'll meet at the overlook, and then drive out to the coast. That's all I know. All I need to know.

***

Lunch is a half hour break divided between shooing out kids and scarfing down food. Once half the camp marches out, the other half is already on its way, queueing up outside along the gate. It's the longest break from the sun we'll get all day. I'm sitting at a table beneath an umbrella across from Machiko, eating my last PB&J when Donny taps me on the shoulder, beckons me to follow. Machiko doesn't say anything, just watches me go. I take the remaining half of my sandwich, follow Donny inside the snack shack through the back door. I try and force it down during the short walk, but my stomach's spinning and I can't manage more than a bite before tossing it in the trash on the way in.

Inside smells of hot dogs and cinnamon candy. The two girls who work the window giggle around a small plastic card table in the back. Brody's finishing some joke, a sleeve of Dixie cups in one hand, a bottle of Fireball in the other. They laugh and turn their attention toward us.

The girls nervously twitch, attempting to hide whatever they're drinking within their small hands. Brody doesn't lose a beat.

"Ready to get fucked up tonight?" he says, giving Donny a fist bump. Whiskey sloshes around inside the bottle.

"He's talking to you," Donny says, taking me by the shoulder and pulling me into their circle. He pulls two cups from the sleeve and tells Brody to pour us some shots. They are uneven; some of the whiskey hits the table between pours. Donny hands me the lighter of the two.

"To hoping the fuckers who run this place die and we never see each other again." We cheers in the center of the table, the girls let out a whoop. The cups tip back, my tongue and throat on fire, worse than the Pixy Stix, and it stays. I'm coughing with the girls. They're smiling, so are Donny and Brody, their glassy eyes. The muscles in my face twitch around a forced grin. Spit floods my mouth and I swallow over and over to keep it all down.

"Another," says Donny. We're all in without argument, our cups back on the table. There's no cheers, no toast this time. Donny downs his as soon as Brody is finished with the pour, and watches as we follow suit. It's no worse than the first. Donny demands another. Brody hesitates; the girls cover their mouths. One more and they'll burst. I set my cup on the table. I'm in.

"'Attaboy." Donny slaps me on the back, hard enough I taste bile on the back of my tongue. Brody's pours are weak and Donny makes him go back over a second time. He waves him off when the cups are half full.

"To tonight." He raises his cup and throws the shot back with a wink. Crunches up his cup, tosses it on the table and marches out alone. That's my cue. I bolt to the sink and gulp water from the faucet. There's a purple water bottle with a faded high school mascot—some kind of vicious cat—in the drying rack on the counter. I don't know who it belongs to, but I fill it anyway. The bell signals the start to the second half of the day, and my body takes an adrenaline dump. I'm shaking as I twist the top of the bottle on. My belly is warm with the liquor, my legs loose and wobbly. The girls are cleaning up the table, stuffing the whiskey in a backpack. I shuffle for the door. I'm going to be late.

"Let's go, kid." Brody holds the door open. He stops me as I try to pass, pressing the water bottle against my chest. The pressure triggers a belch. His face twists into a grimace as he waves away the stench—looks for a second like he might lose it himself. "Keep it together, will ya?"

I blow the last of it out, and pull my shades down. The sun cuts right through.

***

Machiko and I begin the afternoon in the chairs. It will be two hours before I'm back on break. After blowing my whistle and shouting at some kids to quit horsing around, I finally relax and spend the rest of my first shift slouched in the chair. Minutes tick by. I'm not even watching the water. It takes a slap from Machiko against my shin to wake me from my daze for the rotation. I push up from the chair, twist around to plant a foot on the ladder and it hits me. My head spins from the movement, muscles suddenly weak. My foot misses the ladder and I nearly slip backward, wrapping an arm around the chair to prevent a fall. Machiko calls out, ducks around the ladder to help support me. I find the missing rung, plant a foot and slowly make my way down. I'm still dizzy when both feet meet the deck. Machiko's asking me if I'm okay, and I nod but I know I'm not. I push off the stand and stagger toward the locker rooms, waving to the lifeguard who I'm supposed to relieve that I need a bathroom break.

The locker room is cloaked in dark shadow. I rip off my sunglasses and hear them clatter against the floor somewhere behind me. I hurry toward the stalls, punch open the first door to find a clogged mess. The smell hits me as I'm stepping into the second and my stomach lets loose as I'm falling to my knees. Vomit splashes against the floor, over the seat. My chest and back are wracked with pain as the heaving surges through me, compressing me like a vice. It's everywhere. It takes all of my strength to hold myself upright, and all I can think about is the mess and how I desperately want to clean it up. When it finally stops, I gather some of the torn toilet paper from the floor of the adjacent stall and smear it across the toilet seat. It's disgusting. I hear footsteps behind me. I need to get back.

**

My eyes open into the darkness of my pillow. What little light manages to sneak in adds to the pressure building inside my head. I'm lying on my stomach, my arms lifeless at my sides. Everything aches. I run my tongue over my teeth and taste sour toothpaste.

"Hey, loverboy," says a voice.

Machiko? I angle my head out from the pillow, crack my eyelids open to see her sitting in a chair across from me, her feet up on the end of the bed.

"I came to check in on you." She reaches down, digs through her backpack and pulls out one of the books I'd loaned her. "Had to drop these off."

"What time is it?"

"You're right, these aren't half bad. Robots, and all," she says, flipping through the pages.

I struggle to locate a clock. There should be one hanging on the wall but I can't find it. I realize the harsh light is from the fluorescent tubes in the ceiling. That outside the sun has already begun to set.

"Shit!" I push up, scramble off the bed. A dizzying rush of blood sends me crashing to the floor, tripping over my feet. I'm still in my uniform, whistle around my neck. My shirt smells of puke. There isn't time to change. I force shoes over my bare, sunburned feet, and stumble for the door but Machiko pushes off the bed, rolling the chair in front of me.

"Where are you going?"

"You know where I'm going."

"It'll be dark by the time you get there."

"So?"

"You're not going to wander around the woods by yourself."

"Then come with me."

She stares at me for a moment, calm as ever while my mind races around endless outcomes and wonders how I got here and where I'm going and why this matters tome as much as it does, but all at once it's too heavy, pinballing as they do. I open my mouth to yell and she tosses the book to me, catching me off guard. I bobble it before dropping it to the floor. She mumbles *butterfingers* and something else I don't catch, rummaging through her backpack until she finds a small flashlight hidden beneath the books. Pulls it out, gives it an on-off test. It's too bright in the room to gauge if it works.

Outside the cabin is cold and quiet. Music echoes in the distance, voices warbling out of tune. We jog away from the gathering and the main camp grounds, looking for a path that leads into the woods toward the lake and then up into the hills. Machiko calls it out when we reach the tree line. We've missed the opening by fifty yards and have to backtrack along the backside of the cabins. My mouth's all but a dried husk. Machiko's keeping pace beside me. All I hear is the sound of my raspy breath and the thud of my footsteps in the grass. My shirt clings to my back, sweat gathering above my brow to invade my eyes. By the time we reach the fork toward the hills they are on fire. I pull up my shirt and nearly trip wiping it over my face. It's grown dark in the woods, but embers still lurk on the horizon. There's hope. Machiko clicks on the flashlight. She waves it back and forth over the trail looking for pitfalls and roots that snake out from the shadows like swollen veins. They force us to walk the rest of the way, until the rocks overtake them.

I know we're too late before we even emerge from the trees. That no one is there at the top of the bluff. But it takes me setting foot on the rock to realize no one was ever here. That there was no plan to meet. That I'd been lied to.

The day rushes out of me in a heaping sigh. I sit on the ledge, stare off across the valley.

"You knew."

She sits down, slides over to me, brushes the dust from her palms. The words echo inside my head, sharpen, turning inward. *You should have known.*

The last of the sun dies on the horizon, the stars wink into existence. They're so clear up here—out here. Where we say goodbye.

Digging Deep

WE'RE barely home from the hospital when it begins to snow, winds whipping up the kind of full-blown blizzard that will hover over New England for days. Amanda's half-asleep, curled up on the couch holding our baby against her breast. She had trouble latching at first but seems to be getting the hang of it just fine. No thanks to our "personal lactation consultant," the timid post-grad who spent all of five minutes hiding behind her clipboard while Amanda fought back tears, the baby wailing in her arms. It took an old nurse with forty five years on the job, no personal space and a steel grip to get the process going. It hurt to watch. I would have liked her more if she kept her mouth shut.

"Do you think we have enough food to ride it out?" Amanda asks. I nod, tell her I'll go for a walk and pick up a few things just in case. Don't want to lose our parking spot on the street. We're new to Boston, but not that new. Snow emergencies prompt parking bans that push cars from the main arteries into the side streets. You won't get your tires slashed but you can feel the tension soar as the inches pile up.

My back is to her as I stare out the window, nursing a beer. We have a nice view from the second story of a triple-decker—can even catch a glimpse of The Pru now that the trees are bare. The cars and sidewalks are already covered in white, flurries quickly stacking in the cold, foreshadowing the Nor'easter all the kids have been praying for since Christmas. Thinking about the work ahead makes my hands ache even though I've got enough extra-strength Tylenol filtering through my bloodstream to damage my liver. That's what I get for spending two nights on a hospital cot that felt like wet cardboard stacked beneath a thin sheet. A stray cat bolts from down the street, parks itself underneath our SUV. There's the hissing and awful strangled cries over already-claimed territory, but none leave the dying warmth of the engine. There's probably a whole crew lumped together under there. The block is full of them.

"Settle on a name?" I ask.

Amanda hums, says not yet. The tired smile on her face is a step up from the hospital. The downside to Nurse Vice-Grip was her need to offer a suggestion or two during each visit, as if she knew best. Some are on our list, favorites even. If we use them now it's like it wasn't our idea, that we're tied to that old bitch forever. I don't want that. Amanda had cried a lot at the hospital, stressing over the issue. It's better now that we're home.

I finish the beer and take the empty bottle to the kitchen at the back of the apartment, set it on the sink. Amanda doesn't like when I drink without her—I've played sober most of the past nine months—but we've been through a lot. It's real now. I come back with a fresh one and turn on the television. Amanda tells me to turn it off, that we're enjoying quiet time as a family. My dad would've cranked up the volume, but I'm not stubborn like him.

"Just the weather, hun," I say, like it might impact tomorrow's commute. I've got three weeks off and I'm not going anywhere, but work's still on my mind. The guys gave me enough shit for taking time that it'll stick for a few days. Don't put that FMLA on your record, man. Some people just hate their life.

Kate, the morning meteorologist, is working overtime in a parking lot somewhere south of the city, down Route 93 toward the Cape. The wind howls, whipping snow against her. She holds the microphone tight in both hands, her faux fur-lined hood shrouding her face. She's beautiful, even in the midst of the storm. That's why they put her there. The Boston area is set to receive a foot and a half of snow she says, signing off. I grab the remote and fulfill Amanda's wish. We talk about the snow. There's no mention of Kate. Kathryn is a name still in the running. We can't have competition lingering in the air. I tickle her thigh and she swats my hand away, not ready to laugh. The baby's lips pop off Amanda's breast like a suction cup – splick – her eyelids flutter closed. Amanda gives me an eye like it's my fault, the interruption.

"We should get some sleep while we can," she says. I nod, listening to the sound of a plastic shovel striking the sidewalk outside. One of the neighbors is already at it. It gets under my skin, like it's some kind of competition. Half the street is retired with nothing better to do. It could be anyone. A gust of wind swipes the house, rattling the windows. I take a long pull from the bottle; think about crawling under the covers, wrapping my arms around Amanda and never going outside again. But the scrape of the shovel continues and I can't get the asshole responsible off my mind. I mention the quick trip to the store. Amanda's not happy but relents, too exhausted to put up a fight. She passes the baby to me. I cradle her in one arm and help Amanda to her feet. She winces, pressing a palm against her abdomen, her shoulders hunch slightly forward. The toll of the extended labor is still visible. If the baby had held out much longer, the doctor had said, the hospital would have been forced to perform a cesarean. Everyone joked afterward how that must have scared Amanda into one last successful push. It can be funny when everything turns out okay in the end.

Amanda blows out a deep breath. Holds her arms out to receive the baby then pauses, alarmed at how at ease I am. I hide my anxiety well, heart pounding at the fragile state of the small body resting against my chest. I carry her past the nursery into our room to the temporary crib at the foot of our bed. Amanda kisses the baby's forehead before I lay her softly inside. The base of the crib is so low that Amanda has difficulty reaching the bottom. She crawls atop the comforter, exhaustion finally taking its toll. She drifts off the moment her eyes close, curled up on her side out of habit. I untuck the sheets from my side of the bed, folding them over to cover her up. She'll be cross with me when she wakes up for ruining her perfect hospital corner. I skip a last glance, resist the pull to join her, and return to the living room in search of my drink.

Outside it's snowing harder, individual flakes molding into sheets of white. I search for the overachiever but he's hidden by the second floor porch overhang. I polish off the beer in two gulps, set the empty bottle beside the TV, and snag my keys.

Winter has taken up permanent residence in the hall outside our front door, the cold seeping through century-old boards. I slip on an pair of old boots with rubber soles that peel at the toe, and a fleece that I've spent the better part of the past three days in. It still smells of the hospital cafeteria—a place I could do without setting foot in again. Together it's not much but it will get me the two blocks to the bodega and back. A bag of salt rests unopened in a bucket at the bottom of the stairs courtesy of the sisters who live on the third floor. It's a nice gesture but that's all it is—something to help us through the week before the next storm washes it away. I wait for a break in the wind and flip the deadbolt. The lull is short-lived and the door presses hard against me as I pull it open and step out. I have to hold it shut while I lock up.

The street is empty except for the overachiever, zipped up in a heavy blue coat, hood pulled tight over his head. He's a regular on the block, stepping out from the adjacent public housing to dote on his Toyota that rolled off the assembly line when I was in high school. He's finished with the length of the sidewalk from bumper to bumper and has moved onto the car itself. I duck behind a column at the corner of the front porch and watch him swipe the snow from the roof. No matter which way he works the brush, the wind whips the snow back into his face. He covers up with an arm attempting to block as much as he can from swirling inside his hood. The effort is futile, the storm already reclaiming his meager progress at his feet.

I head down the steps, crossing the street to avoid having to cut past the old man. He sees me and calls out anyway. I make out something like, some storm, eh?—I nod out of habit as I head for the store.

Traffic leaving the city is bumper to bumper on South Street. Hours from rush hour and people already heading home to avoid the worst of the weather. A flood of school buses doesn't help, drivers running their routes with a little something extra in their step, trying to get home at a decent time like everyone else. An asshole guns his pickup as I approach the crosswalk, blocking my path. He's riding the van in front so hard that there's not enough space for me to squeeze past. I circle around the back of the truck avoiding his stare, shaking my head. Let him stay hot. Don't have the energy to pick a fight and live it down.

The bodega is another block up South, across from the public housing. Inside I grab cash from a small ATM that takes longer than my walk to spit out. The woman behind the counter barely looks up from her phone. It smells like cats and sure enough, there's a large tabby splayed atop a bag of rice at the end of the cereal aisle. It ignores me as I slip past. I settle for a box of Frosted Wheats. I'm not sure what I came for, other than to get out of the house. The baby was past due. We'd shopped ahead of time, filled the fridge with more food that we could eat before a portion would go bad.

A box of pancake mix and a half-gallon of milk nearing expiration round out my collection. I waffle over the beer lining the fridges along the back until I put it off. Don't want to argue over another six pack. Bigger things to worry about. Like naming our child.

I pay for the groceries with the new twenty, receive mangled bills and a pair of dimes for change. I flatten out the cash on the counter to the annoyance of the woman, fold the wad in half and slip it in my back pocket. She bags the groceries in a small black plastic bag. I drag it off the counter, see the handles stretch gray with the weight. It'll snap before I reach the end of my street. I hug it to my chest and head out into the blizzard.

He's waiting for me, waves as soon as I come into view.

"Hey, my friend," he says, then points to my apartment. "New baby, eh?" His words are confused with a thick accent, but his mention of my daughter raises the hair on the back of my neck. Gets my blood pumping as I cross the street to hear him out.

"What'd you say?" There's anger inside but none registers in my voice. He taps his shovel against the sidewalk dislodging clumps of snow. I hear a newborn cry—she's awake, again. He points again, laughing.

"Two kids of my own. You better get some sleep."

I leave him laughing and tapping his shovel.

The baby's cries fill the apartment. Amanda's got her on the changing table in the nursery, strapping a new diaper on as I walk in.

"What took you so long?" She dismisses the random assortment in my arms. "Take her, will you? I've got to

39

wash my hands."

She flinches away from my frigid palms. I pull the sleeves of my fleece over my hands and carefully scoop her up.

It's a repeat of before, bed for Amanda, beer for me. The old man is gone. A snow plow crawls up the cross-street replacing inches of snow with a layer of salt. The spread is uneven, piles plopping out of the back every few feet.

I kick back on the couch. It's that time of day that sports highlights don't even touch. All of the local stations have replaced their usual programming with storm coverage. It's going to be worse than predicted, a fact they don't miss a chance to play up segment after segment. It all blurs together, then I'm out.

I wake an hour later, kick over the beer I'd set on the floor. I'm lucky it's empty, but my heart still smacks with adrenaline that sets me on edge.

"Someone's hungry." Amanda sits up against a pile of pillows in bed, the baby back on her breast.

"What about you? Pizza?" She blows me a kiss.

The pizza bakes. When I join Amanda in bed she wrinkles her nose and tells me I stink. A hot shower would help loosen my back. Like everything else in the neighborhood, the house is old, and there's no ventilation for the shower. The real estate agent said that a century ago, people took lukewarm baths. Now, if you close the door, the walls sweat fat drops and the air thickens until it's difficult to breathe. Part of me is so tired I fear the heat might knock me out, and she'll find me bleeding out having struck my head on the faucet. I think about this, but I don't mention a word. I want to shovel first.

"Just a few minutes to show we made an effort. Clean off the car in case—"

"What? In case what?"

I realize that I've been staring at the baby, that I'm thinking of all the things that could have gone wrong, could go wrong. I should have stuck with my own death by shower. I kiss her on the cheek and reassure her I just want to be prepared.

My winter jacket hangs in a corner of the baby's room. I have to dig through her closet for my hat and gloves. Amanda's arranged the supplies: diapers, wipes, ointment—you name it—with such perfection that I don't have the heart to mess it up, and by the time I get it all back in place, a timer alerts me to the pizza. I pull on my jacket and hat and pace the perimeter of the kitchen. The oven is fickle, its temperature running ten to thirty degrees above the readout on the dimming display. A lesson learned the hard way when we first moved in with a charred batch of cookies and a house full of smoke. We've been underestimating every meal since. Amanda says to leave her a plate in the kitchen. She doesn't want to sleep in a bed full of crumbs, and when I think about it, neither do I, so I stay in the kitchen and proceed to scorch the roof of my mouth.

It sets me off, the fucking sauce. Amanda says I've got to watch my fucking language—just like that, cursing herself—around the baby. She'll pick up on things as an infant. In the moment all I think about is the pain and how that busted oven makes everything so hot, and next thing I know I've stomped my way outside, shoes buried under six inches of snow, holding a shovel with bare hands. The sun has vanished. The streetlight casts a dull orange glow. I swipe a handful of powder and pop it in my mouth like I'm five years old. It feels good against the burn. I run my tongue over cold melt as I scan the empty street. The overachiever has been at it again, and the neighbor on the right shoveled a narrow strip down the sidewalk to his property line. Footsteps continue past to the end of the block. I start on the porch.

He comes limping up the hill when I'm finishing the stairs. His car has taken on a couple of inches, the drifts covering sidewalk look like he never bothered. It's a free hint to pack it in and go back upstairs, but I'm already committed. He calls out to me, bracing his shovel over a shoulder as he plods up the center of the unplowed street. I can't make out what he's saying until he's two car-lengths away.

"No plows, huh?" I think he's repeating himself. The answer to his question is obvious—he's standing in it. "I see them driving around. They don't pay attention." He gestures toward the cross street, which has been plowed and salted twice since the start of the blizzard. It looks good, but it will be forgotten along with the rest of the side streets when the storm worsens overnight.

"They'll get to it eventually." I shrug, put my head down and go back to work on the sidewalk. It's so light I could sweep it with a broom.

"Not gonna be able to get out of here if they keep this up." He walks around his car to find his work undone, shakes his head. "Snow like this, it just keeps blowing around. I keep shoveling and the guys around the corner do nothing. It's just going to pile up and blow back on my space."

I don't have the energy to argue, or explain that if he wanted less work, he should have parked on the opposite side of the street to avoid the wind making him look like a fool. I find a rhythm, finish the sidewalk in front of the house, even the extra ten feet to his car, linking the two sections. I wave off his thanks, plowing my way across the street to our car. The cold is beginning to creep through my shoes, into my socks. My toes are warm, but my exposed hands are half-frozen, fingers slowing down. They're good enough to grip the shovel and not much else. I shove them in my pants pockets and warm them against my legs for a minute before unlocking the car and getting the scraper out of the back. I'm finishing up the windshield, the wipers skyward so they don't freeze to the glass, when I hear a shout.

It's the overachiever. He's running down the street. I hear the snow plow grinding its way up the cross street and curse myself for setting foot outside. Anxiety swells in my stomach. Any second he's going to bite it and I'll be the one who has to call an ambulance when he breaks a hip. His arms suddenly fly up in panic, his feet sliding as he tries to stop. He snags the door handle of a Jeep parked at the end of the street and somehow manages to stay upright. I exhale, realize I've been holding my breath.

The snow plow is one of the smaller variety—a pickup with a large salt spreader strapped down in the truck bed. The driver sees him and stops, lowers his window. The overachiever gesticulates wildly—one arm drawing circles in the air, rotating at the elbow, the other pointing past me, up and down the street. I can't hear him through the wind, but I know what he wants the driver to do. In years past when storms measured in feet, backhoes were repurposed for the heavy lifting. Sometimes the drivers would back up the street to better clear out the snow. The construction vehicles weigh nearly ten tons, and still they appear to float—even bounce—over the snow.

The overachiever appears proud of himself. He flashes me a smile and a thumbs up as the driver pulls the snow plow past, stops and throws it in reverse. The warning beep echoes off the houses. The maneuver has disaster written all over it. The driver has the correct angle, but he's barely turned the wheel when the rear tires begin to skid. Brake lights flare, the tip of the plow comes within a foot of slicing a parked car. He guns the engines twice. The wheels spin in place, and then drag the truck down. The driver gets his foot back on the break just in time, tires catching on some smidgen of asphalt mere inches from another car. The overachiever starts after him, but the driver gives up and retreats back the way he came. I doubt we'll see him again.

I finish dusting off the rear-windshield, toss the scraper inside and lock up. My throat is parched and I feel the dull throb of a headache developing. I need a drink.

He yells—"Did you see that?"—as I pass. "Asshole just drove off. I'm going to complain." I glance up at him but don't say anything. He follows me down the street, talking to himself—or me, the entire time. I can't quite tell which. I weave through the traffic, the miserable drivers glued to their phones. I tap the snow from my shoes at the stoop of the bodega and step inside.

By the time I settle on a six pack he's got three bags' worth of food on the counter. He eyes my six pack as the woman at the register rings him up, says, "Gotta be prepared, ya know? City's gonna shut down tomorrow." The woman behind the counter says something in Spanish that gets him laughing again.

I suddenly have the need to explain myself, that I've already come once for food. It's embarrassing the way I stumble over words. I sound like him. He wishes me luck, pays and heads back out into the blizzard. I'm sure I'll hear the scrape of his shovel in an hour or two.

Car horns blare outside in response to a driver making a poor attempt at a three point turn. The street is too narrow with cars parked on both sides, turning three into six and blocking traffic. The wind picks up, gusts tearing down the street making it difficult to breathe. I turn around, my back against it—and see the overachiever down on his hands and knees. He'd left heading the opposite direction. At first I think he fell, and then I see the fruit scattered about and the torn bag in his hand. It's obvious as he sifts through the snow that there's too much for him to carry. Amanda's probably wondering where I took off to, but I can't leave him. I pick up a pair of oranges that rolled away from the break and carry them to him.

The look of surprise on his face is bittersweet, like he'd never expect anyone to help him, let alone someone like me. His apartment is just across the street on the second floor of a building shaped like a short L. I help him pile the contents of the torn bag into the two survivors and cross the street, supporting the bottom of the bags with a hand to prevent another disaster. We barely make it to his apartment intact.

Inside is sparse—hotel room sparse, with a hint of disinfectant in the air. I picture him obsessively wiping away dust that accumulates each day. If not for a Puerto Rican flag in the window, and a collection of framed family photos hanging throughout the living room, I'd guess the place to be empty. We set the bags on the kitchen counter and inspect the contents. A fifth of rum and two eggs are the final casualties. He chuckles to himself, referencing my beer as he pours what's left of the rum into a cup, inspecting it for shards of glass. I uncap a bottle of beer and hold it out for him. At first he refuses, but he's quick to give in. I uncap one for myself and we clink, celebrating our small victory. The various photos hanging from the walls are of his family. Here his kids are young, but they're much older now, he says. He hasn't seen them or his wife in a long time. She died of breast cancer three years ago. I watch him crumble as he recounts their stories. All I can do is keep my beer in my mouth and drink. He's barely touched his when I plunk my empty down and take one for the road. I tell him I'll see him around, leave the remainder of the six pack on the table and head out. I can't get out of there fast enough.

I leave through a different door than we came in, nursing the beer. Bass hums from a nearby window. I cut through the playground at the center of the public housing to my street, where I stare at the lights in our house as I make my way up. Amanda's inside with our daughter, swaddled in their respective beds. I imagine the snow

falling for days, trapping us inside. The overachiever—
our neighbor—tunneling his way to his car, clearing his
spot. I listen from the couch, snuggled under blankets
with my family. We're trapped, sure, but it doesn't feel
that way. I pour out the last of the beer, nestle the bottle
within a snow drift, and ascend the steps.

Bringing in the Dead

SERGIO watched through the side mirror as Angel slowly meandered away from the ambulance, shoes scuffed from dragging his heels in an effort to extend the routine. Angel's shoulders slumped, attention focused on the empty plastic bottle that he kicked forward over the cracked pavement every few steps. A large section of the cinderblock wall that framed the left side of the street had been freshly tagged with *CDS*, a mark of the Sinaloa Cartel—thin lines of black spray paint quickly scrawled for message, without any thought for design. Sergio punched the center of the dash and the air conditioner hummed to life. His knuckles began to sweat. It was only a matter of time before the dry heat of the cab would reduce him to using his shirt as a towel. If he didn't get out soon, he'd be forced to dig through his bag in the back for a spare uniform that he may or may not have forgotten, buried under a heap of dirty laundry in his apartment. He let out a long sigh, wondering if his American counterparts across the border suffered the same. *No,* he quickly concluded, *they wouldn't put up with such conditions.* He put the thoughts to bed—the heat was the least of his concerns.

Before he could change his mind, he grabbed the window crank and rolled down the glass. Fresh air flooded the cab, but other than clear out the stench of a warm body, it did little to change the conditions. The side mirror singed his fingers as he bent it outward to observe his partner, giving it a few taps to knock it into place. Angel was still in view, having followed the bottle's path into the middle of the street. Sergio pulled his hand out of the sun and rolled up the window. Nothing had changed.

Church bells in the distance signaled the noon hour. Not even close to the end of their shift and already on their fourth call. When the first came in before they could leave the hospital parking lot—an early morning drunk who put his pickup through the bar he had just stumbled out of—Sergio should have known it would be a long day. The creases in Angel's dry-cleaned uniform showed the strain. Sergio liked Angel's spirit, but the real Ciudad Juàrez was hitting the kid at a pace he could barely handle, the violence threatening to crack the recruit before he could finish his first month on the job. Sergio made a mental note to take him out for drinks when their shift ended. He had failed, again, as a partner and more importantly a mentor, to prepare the young man. If he wanted to maintain a reputation for running a tight shift, he'd have to do better. Angel wouldn't suffer like he did when he first donned the white uniform, that was for sure. In fact, he'd hidden a large jug of pulque beneath the ice packs in the back in case of an emergency. *I think this qualifies.* He licked his lips at the thought. The alcohol was an acquired taste, but one that he was sure the pair would bond over. Like Sergio, Angel became a paramedic to serve the public. But until Angel understood what that service entailed, he was better off killing time by picking up a plate of tacos or cup of coffee. *One day at a time kid, take our time and do it right.* Sergio wouldn't pull out photos of his former partner's tortured body unless Angel threatened to go to their superiors. *It's not corruption when your life is on the line. Think and then act. No white knight bullshit.* But Sergio didn't seriously think it would come to that, not with his guiding hand.

Sergio checked the passenger side mirror. A few drunks brazen enough to wander the streets of Anapra sat on paint buckets grouped together in a sliver of shade that grew with each passing minute. *Good*, thought Sergio. The quiet was comforting, and he was happy to sit for a few minutes after driving in circles, helping the day along by showing Angel the poorer neighborhoods of the city where rich kids didn't tread. He'd pulled the ambulance into the mouth of the side-street at an odd angle to block entry, with just enough room for him to open his door and squeeze through the gap. It wasn't optimal, but they'd been less than a mile away when the call came over the radio. Male victim—another drive-by shooting.

In fact, they had been so close to the scene that it didn't hit Sergio until he locked eyes with the dying man who laid face up in the dust mere yards from the truck. He'd cursed and kissed the crucifix around his neck before jerking the wheel and throwing the stick in park. He flicked the switch to kill the siren and then he and Angel both closed their eyes and said a prayer. It was a tradition that Sergio's former partner had passed on. A small word with God for their safety and a few minutes for the victim's heart to call it quits. Angel finished first, taking a deep breath and placing his hands on the dash as he took in the cartel's latest revenge. He pulled out a clipboard and began the paperwork. From day one, Sergio had given him all of the busy tasks, things to keep his green conscious off the bloody work that lay ahead. Sergio radioed in their impending arrival (ETA five minutes) and sent Angel for coffee. Almost like clockwork. The kid was good and he didn't ask questions—not yet, anyway.

Sergio flipped through the paperwork from earlier jobs: an elderly man suffered a heart attack (kept alive en-route, current condition unknown) and a teenager fractured her ankle on the receiving end of a nasty slide tackle. Simple stuff that was covered well in training. He stole a glance at the red smear drying ahead in the street. *If the kid gets sick again, we are going to have a serious talk. Sure, the real thing is different than theory or dummy practice, but three times? What are they teaching these kids?*

When he processed through, the instructor had surprised the class huddled around a cadaver by taking a machete to the dead man's leg. Sergio would never be able to forget the THUNK of the blade lodging in the femur bone. And then, after the shock of the act died down, he took a hammer to the man's face! *They must be getting off easy these days,* Sergio concluded. He hoped they got to watch the result of serious trauma through a video. It was the least the school could do.

Sergio sucked at his front teeth, the early arrival still

weighing on his mind. It's not that it wasn't manageable (he'd done it before), but he was lead EMT now and little mistakes made him feel like an ass in front of Angel. His cell phone chirped again in his pocket, a second reminder to do his job. No doubt a message passed on from nearby eyes. He clicked off the phone in disgust. How dare they question his commitment? Sure, he had arrived early—mere minutes after the drive-by riddled the SUV. He might have even heard the gunfire if not for the deafness in his left ear, and the blaring of the radio, turned up to compensate for the impairment. Again, he scanned the body that lay still in front of the SUV. Had the man moved? No, he hadn't, though Sergio could tell he was still alive. Years ago Sergio would have had to move closer, maybe even stand directly over the man to properly gauge his condition. He could barely stomach the fact that he had once gone as far as checking for a pulse. Victim still alive? Shit, forgot the equipment back in the ambulance. He'd invented a bad limp or a hernia more times than he could remember to excuse his listlessness between the truck and his duty. And with his bad ear, there was always the chance for poor communication—that he never had to fake.

Sergio worked hard through the nineties, developed the eyesight of a hawk, able to determine the affiliation of the victim from twenty yards away. In this case, a member of the Aztecas. The feathers tattooed on the man's forearm were the indicator. Sergio smiled at that. Where providing medical attention to a rival of the Sinaloa was considered a grave error, it felt good to get something so right. A code of ethics amounted to no more than sticking a gun in your mouth and testing the trigger.

He grabbed a handful of paper napkins from the glove box and wiped them across his brow and the back of his neck, his thinning hair underperforming as usual. The busted air conditioner groaned and shut off despite additional attempts to nudge it along. Heat danced on the hood of the ambulance, the rusting seams and rivets throbbed in tune with the beat of Sergio's heart. He loved his truck so much he'd even contemplated fixing her up with his own savings. But he concluded that would only draw more unwanted attention. A morphine addict with a switchblade hoping for a fix was one thing; a gang looking to boost a 'new' ambulance was another. So he let her age along with himself, their wrinkles becoming more apparent each day.

Just die already. He slapped the wheel for letting the ugly thought come to the forefront of his mind. It was the heat, but he dare not open a window, not even to smoke. A lesson learned the hard way. Families of victims screaming, thrusting arms, fingers, heads at him through the port as he tried in vain to crank it shut. Why won't you save my son/husband/lover? He was saving them, in his own way. But they wouldn't understand, so he kept his windows up and his hands busy.

Angel had disappeared from view, most likely into whatever shop appeared the cleanest on his adventure through the slums. Sergio watched the ticks of the tiny second hand on his watch as it slowly made its way around. He couldn't hear it, but the sound still echoed in his head. *Click, Click, Click.* He could use a cigarette, but trapping himself in with the smoke would only make him feel worse. *Relax, only a few more minutes.* He ran a mental checklist over the console and dash. *Radio back in place, check. Sirens off, check. Lights on, check. Quarter tank of gas—fill up later. Paperwork all set, check.* Then he saw her—*Young female, well dressed, standing over victim, che...*

Too late. Sergio tried to duck down but she was already running toward the ambulance, heels clacking against the pavement, screaming for help. *This is bad. This is very bad.* His only coherent thought on repeat. Before he could radio Angel she had slipped through the gap and had her hands on the locked door. Sergio turned and looked at the woman because he had to—it was only a matter of time before she found a bottle or a good size rock to put through the window. *You're a professional, handle it.*

It sounded like the fallen man was her brother, though he couldn't fully understand through the outpour of emotion. How did he miss her? *I should have caught sight of her green dress when she was blocks away.* Her slender curves and model face didn't belong in Anapra. She was putting herself in danger. The fact that he found himself more worried about her safety than his role in the mess was lost on him. *Help her, Sergio.*

He took a deep breath and opened the door. The woman quieted at the small victory, wiping the smudged makeup underneath her left eye. As Sergio climbed down from the cab, plastic medical kit in hand, her features struck him again. Orange pastel lipstick and a colorful bracelet, a band of bright flowers on her left arm. Where had he seen her before? Another site? Perhaps, but he didn't think that was right. He would have remembered her face, her tenacity.

As soon as his feet hit the ground she grabbed his arm, her nails digging into his slippery wrist, pulling him with all the strength her small frame could muster.

"Help him, he's dying!"

"I know, that's why I'm here. I'm here..." The words trailed from his mouth. Her strong pull overwhelmed the false pains in his knee. The medical kit cracked against the truck as she dragged him through the gap, cement wall scratching his back through his shirt. He was more prepared for a backyard tea party than the bloody crime scene. Gauze and bandages for stuffed animals, sick from too many cookies. He used his weight to try and slow her down, to catch his breath. He'd lost control of the situation. He couldn't suck enough air into his lungs to think of a solution and in the confusion, his act caught up with him.

He tripped over a divot in the road, the kit flying wide, palms and knees eating gravel, taking the brunt of the fall less than a foot away from the dying man. Sergio caught himself before face planting, his palms coming up gooey with blood. It was everywhere, the crimson lake baking at Sergio's knees as he sat on the edge. He couldn't believe the man was still breathing. His shirt and right leg were soaked through, to the point where Sergio had difficulty determining how many times he'd been hit. And there were no tattoos, just swirls of blood mixed with dirt. He rubbed his eyes. *Where are the feather tattoos? How could I have been mistaken?* He fumbled for the kit—but the woman was quicker, retrieving it with emergency speed. But she didn't hand it to Sergio. Instead, she pointed over his shoulder and yelled.

Angel had returned. The prodigal son stacked two large drinks on the hood of the truck and sprinted towards the trio. Sergio's phone chirped, sending his heart into such a fury that he thought he might be having a heart attack. He threw up his arm like a gate in front of Angel as he crashed down.

"Get the trauma pads," said Sergio, though it came out in a mumbled gibberish and he had to repeat himself twice before Angel took off towards the truck. Sergio's hands shook uncontrollably. Angel couldn't be allowed to see this, the desperation that had overtaken his every move.

The man's chest twitched with each shallow breath. Sergio slid over to the man's head, rolling it up and then tilting it down to tighten his wind pipe. He tried to steady his nerves but there wasn't any time. The woman clutched the red kit to her chest.

"Checking for air", he mumbled aloud. It was now or never. There was no room for error. The man's breath felt cool against his cheek as he hovered, bent over. Then down in a fluid motion, thumb plugging the man's nose, hand holding the head in place and fitting the fat of his cheek over his mouth. It only took seconds—a little more than the amount of time it should take to tell if there was any breath left. By the time Angel returned, Sergio was sitting back on his knees.

"He's gone."

The woman collapsed over the body in tears, wiping the bloody smudges from the man's face that Sergio had left behind. Angel stood next to the gurney, thick trauma pads in hand.

"Should I make the call?"

"No," said Sergio, "Let's take this one back. It's not safe for her to be in the neighborhood. We've done enough waiting today." He stood and dusted off his pants, taking a moment to collect himself and let any tears roll back into their ducts before turning to Angel. They donned latex gloves and together lifted the dead man and strapped him onto the gurney. Angel rolled him to the waiting ambulance while Sergio escorted the woman. He couldn't get much out of her. She didn't have a car and was fine to ride in the back.

He paused before getting into the cab. The cola Angel brought back was lukewarm, but he could still taste the diluted sweetness. He chewed on the straw and stared at the SUV. His phone chirped again. *What a waste.* He threw the cup on the ground and climbed inside.

Angel updated their status over the radio, his voice stronger and more confident than Sergio anticipated. Perhaps Angel had learned something. There was a lesson to learn here, though Sergio wasn't sure what it was. By the time he threw the stick in reverse, the sweet taste of the drink had bittered in his mouth. He flipped on the siren and gunned it for the highway. Several blocks later they hit the lunch traffic. Angel flicked the siren to gain attention but the parking lot ahead of them only continued its crawl. Drivers were always slow to react to emergency crews, especially EMS, who wouldn't be pulling anyone over and forcing them to open their wallet or face a ticket. Men with sticks of hanging fruit wandered in-between cars, dragging coolers behind, looking for a few pesos from those whose hunger or thirst got the best of them.

A short man wearing a Yankees ballcap waved a stick of whole pineapples over the hood of the ambulance, their stems woven together with thick strands of rope. Sergio waved his hand and blared the horn until the man gave up and moved to the next car. As he passed the front of the ambulance a city bus merged over, cutting Sergio off. Enraged, he slammed down the horn, its growl lost in the sea of traffic.

Angel looked out the window. He cracked his knuckles, his newly found confidence waning as he grew unsure of what to do next. *Be the mentor Sergio, talk to him and open his eyes.* The words were lost on the tip of his tongue. There was no way to express the full extent of the danger they faced, no way to rationalize it. Sergio collapsed back into his seat, defeated. "Ah, well," he said. *At least the man is dead.* That was something he could take comfort in. There would be time to review the day with Angel once things died down at the hospital. He flicked the siren again as he pressed closer to the bus.

"Christ!" He started at the sight of the woman's eyes, magnified. Her portrait emblazoned on the rear of the bus in an advertisement for the Channel 4 News. That's where he'd seen her! She anchored the evening news, famous for her tough investigative reporting on corruption within the city.

By the time he realized the last run was more than a gang hit, the bullets were punching through the hood, trailing upward through the windshield and into his chest. Two men emptied full magazines from their assault rifles and took off at a sprint through the maze of traffic. As the world dimmed around him, Sergio thought of the woman. Maybe, in some way, he had saved her too.

The siren continued to wail, its cry mostly ignored, background static to those just trying to make their way home.

Lupe's Lemon Elixir

RAUL doesn't ask for favors. He delegates.

Lupe assumes it's because he's finally risen to the top of the cartel. The "business" side, that is—more money, less guns and drugs. Maybe their divorce propelled him over the hump—fewer people around to ask questions, though she made a point not to during the last fifteen years. A good man can be hard to find in this town, her mother had said, offering Lupe's father and uncles as evidence. She didn't doubt it was true.

Delegate, that's what you do when you're the boss; Raul used to tell her when they'd argue over the cleaning business. Her response: One van, two ladies. That's how it had always been, with her mother and her grandmother before. Family was the reason they'd been the most sought-after cleaning crew in all of Mexico City for decades. That, and a best kept secret, but Raul didn't need to know about that. The husbands never knew.

"Raul doesn't ask for favors." She says it aloud this time, but not loud enough for her niece, Ana, to hear over the squawking of the radio. A DJ shouts through the speakers, informing her of the traffic conditions in

Mexico City: poor. Her firsthand exposure confirms worse—and the smog-tainted heat they'll be enjoying from the late morning on won't make it any better. She finds herself nodding in agreement, wishing her cold coffee contained a pinch of whatever keeps the man in some far-off radio station dancing through the early morning hours. She feels for the cross hanging from her necklace. Rubs the smooth metal between thumb and index finger. Ana stretches like a cat in the front passenger seat, her yawn leaving behind ghostly condensation against the side window.

"Why did we have to come out so early?" she asks, pulling her feet up onto the seat, knees against her chest; a nineteen-year-old child. "Mom's going to be grouchy all weekend thanks to you."

"Your mother hasn't slept in since the day you came into this world. Another hour and she'd be up making breakfast for your father and tidying the house," says Lupe. "The world keeps spinning while you night owls are off in dreamland."

Ana rolls her eyes as if signaling Lupe's fall from Cool Aunt to a carbon copy of her mother. She reaches out, pressing her hands against the dashboard vents, the sleeves of her sweatshirt pulled up over her fingers. "There's no heat."

"Hush," Lupe says, cuffing Ana's arm with the back of her hand. "It'll be 90 by noon and you'll be complaining about the busted AC and how your skin is sticking to the seat."

A cab cuts in front of Lupe and she jams her foot on the brake. Slaps the horn and curses the driver from within the van. He taps a cigarette out the window. He doesn't look up.

"What a jerk," says Ana. A long, pink and gray nail file appears out of thin air. Ana goes to work gracefully buffing and polishing until her fingers shine with perfection. Lupe glances at her own gnarled hands clutching the wheel. Blue-green veins are visible beneath taught skin that's a pale shade lighter than the rest of her body. She should have worn gloves when she was younger, the acidic cleaners leaving her palms permanently dry and cracked. Decades of demand had turned her soft touch to rough tree bark. Ana had called her Mummy Hands when she was younger, wrapping them in toilet paper for Day of the Dead.

"Speaking of…" says Ana, pausing to slip a sideways smirk at her aunt, "How's Uncle Raul?"

Lupe thinks back on the anxiety in his slur-tinged voice. He'd called three times before the endless vibration knocked her phone from the nightstand to the floor, startling her awake. The alarm clock had read just after midnight, but when she saw his name lit up on her phone, it felt more like two; a very exhausted two.

"Oh, I suppose he's doing fine and making the most of his bachelorhood," Lupe tells Ana, though she doesn't believe the words. It's no surprise that Raul had called her drunk but the urgency in his voice, the request for a *favor*, was new. He needed her *now*, and she'd been quick to remind him it was the first time she'd heard that since their honeymoon.

"It's not life or death," she'd joked, and when he didn't respond, she remembered everything was life or death in the drug trade.

"We're not doing this for free, are we?" says Ana, with the serious concern of a teenage girl.

"Raul had to leave the city early, but left a little something in the apartment for us."

"A little something?"

Lupe shrugs. She's focused on calculating how much time they'll have before they need to leave for their first scheduled appointment. Traffic continues to crawl, shaving off minute after minute. Timing is everything.

"Good," says Ana, turning her attention back to her nails. *Good*, thinks Lupe. If only everything could be wrapped up in a single word. "What's the emergency? New girlfriend moving in?"

Ana's chin droops to her knees and she looks away out the window in silence. Lupe senses her regret, but she doesn't apologize. Apologies have never been her thing. She slips her smart phone out from her purse and taps a message to a friend. A minute later and she's checked out. She could be anywhere.

***

They crawl bumper to bumper for thirty minutes before the traffic jam finally dissolves from the haze of exhaust as if it never existed. The van rattles as Lupe presses her foot against the accelerator, wrenching its pistons from their nap. She remembers the leak and reminds herself to pick up a quart of oil.

A luxury high-rise blooms beside the highway in the distance, its steel and glass curves bronzed by the morning sun. The apartments within are the kind Lupe would only get a glimpse of on the job, mopping the floors and dusting the sills of the richest families in all of Mexico. Of course there were Cinderella-esque dreams of inhabiting the fairy tale life, but those ended quickly when she was young and her mother caught her playing Goldilocks in the beds of a government official's home. Trust is everything.

Raul's apartment is on the 25th floor. The speed and ease at which he moved in makes her realize he'd already had it. He'd handled their finances when they were together, but aside from the occasional expensive watch—Raul loved his time pieces—she would never have considered them wealthy. If she gave it some thought she could piece it together but she has a chin to keep up and a business to run.

They trade the highway for a bottleneck of city traffic. Lupe runs fingers through lengths of her hair, twirling the tips against her jaw. A nervous tic she picked up from her mother. Ana breaks her silence to ask Lupe what's the matter and she ignores her. They need to be across the city in less than two hours if they are to stay on schedule. That should still give them plenty of time to take care of a small apartment, but Lupe has no idea what kind of dirt she's getting herself into. Last minute calls are guaranteed to get messy.

Ana exhales a long sigh, leans her head against the window. Lupe feels the weight of her niece's boredom on her shoulders. With no children of her own, she's lucky to have someone interested in carrying on the family tradition. Maybe she'll take her out shopping later and buy her something nice with the extra money from Raul.

Lupe taps her fingers against the steering wheel. Only blocks away from their destination. She can no longer see the top of the tower, even when she cranes her neck. They are that close.

There are signs lining the street that say NO PARKING, but Lupe checks her side mirrors and pulls over anyway. The tires on the right side of the car hop the curb of the sidewalk with ease. When she's confident she's not blocking traffic, she pulls the parking brake and shifts to park.

Ana asks her if she's sure about this. "Yes," she says, she'll fold in her side mirror.

The air has warmed up outside. Lupe opens the back of the van. Ana reaches inside and retrieves the vacuum, draping the tubing over her shoulders. The cord is wrapped tight against the body of the vacuum, just as she's been taught. Lupe places a backpack and a five-gallon bucket full of supplies on the street. As she locks up she looks around for police but doesn't see any. She crosses her chest and prays they stick to traffic problems.

A handsome doorman dressed in a suit of maroon and gold holds the door open with hands gloved in white. His smile takes a giggle from Ana as they pass into the lobby. Lupe's mother would've snapped at her for such a reaction. Part of their job is to be invisible. But Lupe doesn't tell this to Ana; If she wasn't so concerned about the time, she thinks she would have smiled too.

The door closes, sealing off the outside noise as they take in the opulence of the small lobby. A leather couch that looks uncomfortably low to the ground is paired with a coffee table carved in the shape of a leaf. The room is filled with the sound of running water from a fountain cascading along the wall adjacent to the elevator bank. A man in similar uniform, minus the warmth, sits behind a desk in the far corner. Lupe leads the way, her footsteps echoing off the marble tile floor. His blank face watches them as they cross the lobby. He stands only when they reach the desk.

"For Señor Gomez?" he asks. Lupe nods yes, fighting to keep her attention on the man's face. There's a slight discoloration halfway down his tie; a dry blotch that bleeds onto his shirt. He's tried to rub it away but his attempt only made it worse. She resists the urge to tell him she can clean it. His eyes twitch. He glances past them, outside, then walks around the desk and instructs them to follow. An elevator is waiting. He blocks the door with a foot and stretches inside the car to swipe a card. A light flashes green and he punches the button for the 25th floor. The door tries to shut on him, bouncing against his foot. He looks at it annoyed, and sighs heavily as if it's the hardest thing he's done all morning. Lupe thinks maybe he's worked the overnight and is counting the seconds until he finishes his shift. Perhaps one of the more wealthy tenants noticed the stain as well and scolded him for his carelessness. It's difficult to take a man seriously who can't maintain a clean household, let alone a shirt. Anyway, that's what her mother said; one of her selling points for the service. A clean home is a happy home.

He digs through a pocket on the inside of his jacket and hands Lupe a key with rough edges that feel freshly cut. Tells her to return it when they are done. He smiles at Ana. When she doesn't laugh he covers the stain with a palm and leaves them alone.

The doors close with a *clunk* and the elevator accelerates quickly. For a half-second the pressure makes it difficult to breathe. Headline news flashes on a small screen in the corner of the elevator. The NASDAQ is up. Two die in a fifty car pile-up in Indiana. Lupe has never been to the United States. There is no mention of Mexico.

The hairs on the back of Lupe's neck stand up as the elevator slows its approach, sending a shiver down her spine, sparking out along her fingers and toes. The sudden shock jars the synapses in her brain and she remembers she is supposed to have come alone. Raul had repeated his request—or was it an order?—multiple times, making it abundantly clear that Lupe was the only one he could trust on such short notice. Groggy from being woken in the middle of the night, Lupe had barely listened to his vague plight—until Raul mentioned payment. Five thousand US dollars was an unimaginable fee, so much that it made Lupe chuckle in disbelief when she made him repeat it. A silence followed in which Lupe thought one or both of them had fallen asleep.

"I wouldn't call if this was something I could take care of myself," he'd said, taking a deep breath. "I need you."

Need me? Laughter burst from Lupe's chest. Better words hadn't been spoken in the last ten years of their marriage. Lupe accepted through tears, hanging up as the laughter transitioned to a coughing fit. It was only later, lying in bed attempting to soak up a few more precious minutes of sleep before beginning an extra-early day that she began to worry about her schedule. But the money was good, she told herself, everything would be okay. She knew better than to ask questions. As in their previous life together, the less she knew, the better off she was. It's the half-truths that bit her in the end, when divorce raised its ugly head, but half-truths are hard to shake.

She'd left her apartment with a theory that her ex-husband was attempting to make up for the financial burden of the separation, but as the elevator halts at the 25th floor, she can't brush aside the feelings that something has gone wrong. Nothing good can come from being alone.

There's a beep and the doors open to an intense aroma of lilacs and vanilla. Ana covers her nose and mouth with a sleeve of her sweatshirt to stifle a cough. "My God," she says, muffled under the sweater, "That better not be coming from his room." She continues but Lupe can't make out the rest over the growing concern filling her head, questioning what she's been dragged into; what she's dragged Ana into. She wills her feet to move before the doors close. They shuffle like they're weighed down with blocks of concrete, the sound of them pounding against the floor with each step reverberating inside her skull.

"What's his apartment number?" Ana says. She's dragging the vacuum down the hall by the handle, pausing by each set of doors and looking them over. Aside from the gold-colored numbering on each door, nothing personalizes the hallway. Lupe follows Ana down the hall past two apartments before she checks the tag attached to the key.

"2519," Lupe says. They realize they are going the wrong way and double back. The smell clings to them.

It's impossible to avoid.

"Do you think he's got a corner spot?" Ana says.

"I hope not," Lupe says.

"Insult to injury?" Ana says.

"No," Lupe says, taking a second to think. Her shoulders are beginning to ache from the weight of the cleaning supplies. "It would take too long to clean. We're barely squeezing him in as it is."

It's close; the apartment one off from the south-east corner. Lupe estimates the location will save twenty to thirty minutes. She clings to hope that they can finish on time. Her backpack slides off her shoulder as she fishes in her pants pocket for the key. The liner sticks against her sweaty palm. She wonders why she put it back in her pocket after reading the apartment number. Finally she yanks it out, the tip snagging on the liner and causing a tear. It's nothing she can't fix but she curses her clumsy fingers, giving them a shake as if they've been wounded.

The fit of the key is tight. The teeth rumble against the deadbolt lock as she slides it in. It sticks and she has to fiddle with it to get it to turn. Ana fidgets quietly behind her as she struggles. Finally Lupe puts her shoulder into the door and the lock pops. The door's not open two inches before more of the pungent vanilla and lilac scent bursts from the room, flooding the hallway. It's even more intense than before, but that's not what catches Lupe's attention. Her nose is switched off at this point, her brain's entire focus rerouted to eyes and the signals they are receiving: wispy splotches of dark red highlight against the white of the back wall like a painter's mistake, an erroneous flick of a wrist. Dark stains on the area rug and coffee table that might pass for shadows if not for the sun streaming in through the bay windows. She hears Ana gasp and worries she's seen it too. Ana calls out to Lupe but her ears are switched off. She pulls the door shut but it's too late now, she seen too much. Others, the bitter concierge, the smiling attendant, know she's seen it too. She lowers her head, pressing it against the intersection of the door and the jamb. The key is stuck in the lock beneath her nose. Stuck, she thinks, just like her. The thought makes her chuckle.

"Lupe," Ana says, louder now, tapping her aunt on the shoulder for the third time.

"What?" Lupe says, pushing off the door. Her voice makes her sound more upset than she means. She frowns, shaking her head. "What's wrong?"

"That smell is what's wrong," Ana says. "I can't go in there. The hallway is bad enough."

"Right," Lupe says. The gears in her head are whirring, clicking away, and processing nothing. "Okay."

"What do you mean, okay? Don't you need me to finish the job?" Ana lifts up the vacuum as if to demonstrate her capabilities. "Offer me hardship pay or something?"

"Hardship pay?" Lupe says. She's never thought about the concept before. It's certainly something her mother never would have entertained.

"Yeah, you know, a little something extra to suffer through it," Ana says, rubbing the tips of her fingers together. It's clear she wants a raise, but Lupe doesn't get it. She's thinking about Raul, and the blood, and who else knows, and what if the men downstairs are in on it, and what if men from the cartel show up, and what if she's late to her next appointment, and what if traffic is bad, or if their van gets towed and—

"Lupe?" Ana says, waving a hand in front of Lupe's face, interrupting her blank stare.

"It's nothing," Lupe says. She scratches at the back of her neck, somehow embarrassed; she's not sure why. "I'm just worried about the van. Could you go stay with it?"

Ana shrugs her shoulders with indifference. Her posture says *I told you so*, but she takes the keys to the van without complaint. Lupe thanks her, watches her go.

She takes a deep breath, opens the door and quickly steps inside, locking the dead bolt. Her heart hammers against her rib cage. The clock is ticking, but she's a pro. It's just her and the room now. She flicks the nearest bank of light switches, fully illuminating the kitchen and living area. The candle burns between an empty bottle of scotch and a stack of cash atop a long table on the far side of the apartment. There's no body—not that she can see anyway. The revelation brings a strange sense of calm to her nerves, and she feels herself becoming more comfortable with the setting. The specs of blood dotting the cream-colored sofa and the wall behind are real now, there's no denying it. Her intense focus zooms out from the couch and she realizes it—the blood—is everywhere. When cleaning is your life you notice everything, down to a rogue grain of beach sand smuggled home from vacation. The large blotch on the rug next to the coffee table is the least of her worries. Lupe attempts a quick mental checklist: couch—two out of three cushions, back; area rug; coffee table—surface and two legs; closet door handle… as the list grows she feels overwhelmed. It's too much to take in all at once. Understand what you're up against and take it one step at a time. She sets her cleaning supplies down on the kitchen floor and lifts her cross to her lips, thanking her mother for her wisdom.

Gloves. Gloves are first order of business. Lupe dumps the contents of the bucket onto the kitchen floor. A pair of yellow rubber gloves is uncovered at the bottom. She tugs them on over her damp hands, releasing the rubber with a snap past each wrist. Faint stains of blood dot in and around the kitchen sink. The taps, faucet, basin; nothing is spared.

And Raul was always so neat and tidy. Very unlike him, she thinks as she unzips her backpack, removing a small, clear soap bottle filled with a neon-yellow liquid. She imagines whatever occurred must have been traumatic, but what if she had blown him off? The condition of the apartment was beyond careless. He could have made a little effort before leaving the mess in her lap.

Lupe runs the hot tap, testing it with a finger until she feels the heat through the glove. She swivels the faucet to the left basin to place the bucket in the right before drawing it back. As it fills she takes the bottle with both hands and holds it upside down above the bucket. She counts out loud to three. The neon concoction oozes into the water, thick as molasses. It's no more than a tablespoon, but that's all she needs to clean the entire apartment. She looks over her shoulder at the large blotch on the rug and adds a fourth just to be sure. She can hear her mother scolding her for wasting "the elixir" as she called it, their family's secret recipe that could penetrate the worst stains and leave the underlying surface looking good as new. Suds form as the water continues to rise, releasing a pleasant fresh lemon scent that cuts through the candle's offensive chemical odor. She crosses the apartment to blow it out, but the coat closet and its bloody door knob give her pause. More details are visible now that she's closer—a smear higher up across the edge of the door and frame; a faint pink on the wall beside the closet, like someone might have braced a hand or arm against it. Raul grabbing something from within or… *putting something within.*

She leaves the candle alone and buries the thought. There's a folded piece of paper on top of the stack of one hundred dollar bills. Inside all it says is THANK YOU. It's barely legible. She doesn't have time to count the cash, assumes it's the right amount—for now. He'll get a piece of her mind when she calls him later. She takes the money and the note and stuffs them inside her backpack beneath the bottle of elixir and a pair of towels.

Lupe plucks a rag from the overturned pile on the kitchen floor, dips it in the bucket. She crosses the coat closet off her mental list, wiping down the adjacent wall, over the ridges of the frame, and in and around the knob. The metal shines as if she'd spent fifteen minutes buffing and polishing. Curiosity of her youth flutters in her stomach. The kind that found her opening jewelry drawers and running her fingers over pearls when her mother wasn't looking. That part of her wants to open the door. An older, wiser part of her doesn't, one that knows some doors once open can't be shut. She gives the knob one last rub, lets it be, then shuts the tap and carries the bucket half-full into the living room, setting it down on the glass coffee table outside of the splash zone. A large clock on the wall tells her she has forty minutes.

The couch is first. Each red speckle comes clean with a dab and a quick scrub. The wall is next, though the streaks take longer to clean and are harder to follow toward the tail end of the drip, and Lupe has to slow down in order to not miss any. The splotch stares at her back as she cleans. It looks like more of a pool or a lake up close, dark and rich enough to have bled through the carpet and onto the hardwood floor beneath. *Maybe it's dripping into the apartment below.* I'm going mad, she thinks. She should have tackled the larger task first and its presence continues to irritate. Finally she leaves the wall behind unfinished to eliminate the annoyance. She's bested some heavy red wine stains in her day, but nothing like this. The top layer is dry and crusty at the edges. She pokes it gently, her index finger punching through to a moist layer beneath. It reminds her of a chocolate lava cake.

Twice she wrings out the rag over top of the stain. Switching to a thick sponge, she rakes it over the surface with two hands, first around the edge then straight through the center. Pink clumps of suds bubble up from the rug, growing with every scrub. For a moment doubt lingers in her mind, but then she can see hints of the carpet coming clean underneath and scolds herself for doubting her abilities. She doubles down, dunking the sponge back into the cleanser, squeezing more of the liquid over the stain and scrubbing hard. The pink suds increase until they form a colossal mound, covering the remainder of the stain. Lupe spreads out the rag and scoops the bubbles on top of it. Carefully she wraps the bubbles up and carries them to the sink.

She's rinsing the rag, watching the suds disintegrate in the drain when there's a knock at the door. It's soft at first. The second knock comes like a fist hammering through the door and it makes her heart jump in her chest. Ana calls out to her from the other side. This causes Lupe to relax a bit, but not fully. The strong knock isn't like Ana.

"One minute!" she says. The apartment is still a mess, the main event half finished. She gives her gloved hands a good rinse in the sink and shakes off the excess water before approaching the door and undoing the deadbolt. She doesn't think to check the peep hole until it's too late. It's only Ana, she repeats to herself. She'll have to grow up one of these days.

Only it's not. Lupe looks up to see a hulking police officer looming over her. He's easily a foot taller or more. The scowl on his face has the look of permanence. His broad shoulders seem to go on forever, cloaked in a cloud of cigarette smoke and spiced cologne. Ana's hands are nervously clasped in front at the waist. She stares at her feet.

"You the owner of the van illegally parked outside?" It carries the weight of an accusation more than a question. The officer's eyes spend half a moment on Lupe. Not even a full sentence. He's pulling the door wide and stepping past Lupe into the room before she can cough up the first word of an excuse.

"My guys want to have it towed," he says. His eyes flash to Lupe on the word towed. Her reaction, the desperation in her face, telegraphs everything he wants to know. If she wants the van in one piece, it's going to cost her. She thinks about the stacks of money in her backpack. Would it be enough? She could buy a new van with that kind of money.

"Some party last night, huh? You know the owner?" he says, inspecting the room. His right hand rides on his hip above the butt of his holstered pistol. Ana emits a horrified gasp two steps into the room. Her eyes are wide in shock, hands covering her mouth and nose. Lupe grabs hold of her, digging her nails into her arm, willing her to be quiet.

The officer wrinkles his nose at the candle. "You light this?" Lupe and Ana both shake their head no.

He squats down, poking a finger into the clean section of the stain. He runs a thumb along the finger, brings it to his nose. "Lemon?"

Lupe nods. The officer's shoulder radio crackles to life. He cranks down the volume, pushes off the table to his feet. Both of his knees pop. He ducks his head into the bedroom. Nothing of interest registers on his face.

"Key to the apartment?" Lupe points to the key lying in the kitchen. He plucks it from the countertop and examines the key.

"Wait here." His tone is even, lacking of threat, but Lupe knows it's there. He can afford it given his size and position. When the door closes Ana bursts into tears. She buries her head against Lupe's shoulder, apologizing profusely for failing to move the van. She should have taken it into the lot, or found an opening further down the street. She's a poor driver but she could have done it. If only, if only, if only. Lupe wraps her arms around her and whispers love into her ear. It's okay, she hears herself say, but she knows it's not. She's barely holding back tears of her own. She's furious with Raul for putting her in this position, furious with herself for accepting and dragging Ana into the mess.

Lupe takes a tall glass from a kitchen cabinet and fills it with cold water. Ana takes small sips, stares at the black and gray patterns in the marble. Lupe's past the stage of paralysis, on autopilot now. She hovers over the stain, takes the sponge and dispassionately scrubs at the edges, working her way toward the streak she cut through the center. After a minute Ana comes over to watch. She asks if it's blood. Lupe barely nods, continues to scrub. Ana chuckles at the insanity of it all.

"Did you know?"

Lupe shakes her head. The pink suds are beginning to pile up again. Two-thirds of the stain has disappeared. She keeps at it, wiping the excess bubbles aside. Only a sliver remains when she hears the door click open. So close with fifteen minutes to go. Might have even finished with time to spare.

The officer is alone. He carries a duffel bag in his left hand. He tells Ana to have a seat. She does.

"That stuff really works then?" he says, acknowledging Lupe's progress on the stain since he left.

"Yes," she manages to say through her parched throat.

"How?" he asks.

"Family recipe," Lupe says.

He cracks a smile at that. Like the suspense is all a big joke. He places the duffel bag on the coffee table next to the bucket and unzips the bag. "You want your van?"

He pulls out a crumpled uniform similar to the one he's wearing, a towel and white undershirt. The uniform it too dark to immediately notice, but the crimson stains on the undershirt and towel are unmistakably familiar. "I need a favor."

Lupe lets out a deep breath, and laughs. Tears roll down her cheeks. The officer's cheeks bloom red, then he's laughing too, and so is Ana.

"Yes," Lupe manages through the laughter. She tells him to have a seat. He does.

Vacation Package

CHEN waited in one of two designer fiberglass chairs facing a modern desk, floor-to-ceiling windows and city skyline beyond. The city that had taken them in, given them work and a place to stay, had once called in a favor. Now it was calling again.

He briefly pondered the number of zeroes on the price tag attached to the view. Wondered how much of the tab the city was on the hook for. His hands lay powerless in his lap. Decades of hard work in local government, and still he was unable to discard the shackles of his parents' undocumented status. From plowing the streets in the winter, to organizing voter programs and working with troubled teens, Chen had given his life to the city. It was all he knew, all his family knew. He'd risked everything for this place, his home.

And now his struggle out of poverty had led him to the spartan office, full of advanced polymers and sleek metals. The setting was in stark contrast to his father's experience, back in the days of worn leather wingbacks, earthy cologne and pine. As his mother would say, "same same, but different."

He missed the sweet scent of tobacco that had clung to his father during their last embrace, before he sat his son down on a bench in City Hall and entered that smoke-filled room, resigned to assuming the misdeeds of another. It was only wire fraud; he'd gotten off easy. Easy if that had been the end of it. The stint was supposed to be temporary, but a bad case of tuberculosis took him before he could serve more than a year. Tough luck, they said. He would have come home with a nice pension. It took years for Chen's anger with his parents to fade, but he knew if his father had ignored the message, it would have put them in the crosshairs for deportation. Now the threat was worse.

Behind Chen, the heavy glass door clicked shut, signaling the beginning of his sentence.

"I appreciate you coming in today." Duffy circled around the table, filling the room with an acrid smell of spiced body spray. Baby-faced and entitled, the new power crop. Chen knew the type all too well. "You know how much the mayor appreciates this. How much the city appreciates your sacrifice in the interest of order."

Right, sacrifice. If only it was mine to freely give. Chen looked down at the polished floor, noting the scuffmarks along the insides of his shoes. His immediate family knew nothing of the matter. He'd hidden the shame and secret well, but the extended effort to do so made his presence in the office only hurt more. Time wrapped around his heart like a vice, squeezing with each passing second. Duffy plopped into his chair, pulled a manila folder out of a side drawer and laid it on the desk.

"Bourbon? Might be appropriate given the circumstances." Duffy chuckled, taking a swig from a water bottle.

Chen closed his eyes, letting the tears sting.

"Sorry, thought a bit of humor might grease the skids. I drew the short straw to be the bearer of bad news."

"Tell me what happens next."

Duffy flipped open the folder, drew a pen from his shirt pocket and ran it along the length of the page before setting it down. "First, let me reassure you that Marissa and the kids will be taken care of while you're away."

The "kids." Asshole doesn't even know their names.

They'd agreed to put off having children until Marissa could establish her consulting gig. But it was slow going, and it tore at Chen to watch his wife flounder in a depression between career and family. So he called in a few favors, let the city remember what his father had done for them, what he was prepared to do for them. A few arms were twisted and as a result, business boomed. Chen buried the secret of his wife's success under years of happiness, finally catching his elusive American Dream.

Until they took him aside and gave him a little reminder of their need for a man to take a fall. Showed him the evidence of corruption, the kickbacks and how easily they could tear his wife down. Chen was pushing forty-five with a pair of three-year-olds, Karen and Grace. His little ladies. Their smiles would haunt him in the darkness of his cell.

"Now, in return for your full cooperation, the package includes…."

The package. Chen chewed on his cheek as the kid sold him a deal on the vacation package of a lifetime. He stopped listening when Duffy dug into the details of the incident. Caught some of the buzz words—DUI, vehicular assault, gross negligence, property damage, fleeing the scene—the details didn't matter. A stand-in guilty plea was on order to maintain the status quo. The name of the actual offender was omitted, of course. He'd never know the identity of the official whose sins he was called to own. Maybe the police commissioner, one of the mayor's top aides. The crime rate was one of the pillars in the coming election. The race was close, and a bit of drunken drama could swing votes. He shifted in his seat, the awkward angles uncomfortable against his back.

A gray bird with flecks of white along its breast stole his attention as it struggled in the high winds outside the building. If only he possessed the courage to fight, a sliver of the will that had pushed his father to smuggle him and his mother from China into the U.S. to avoid persecution. Life is a constant struggle, his father used to say. But a man could only do so much.

The bird turned its head and dove.

Beyond the Sea

BOBBY tip-toed out of the motel room, the pockets of his swim trunks full of salt water taffy, fingers sticky from unwrapping Dolle's finest. The door clapped shut behind him, muffling the coin-op television, the booming laughter of evening game shows which drowned out the ocean and lulled his mother to sleep. At home Bobby would simply close his bedroom door to escape from his mother's routine, but their stay in Ocean City left him with no other option than to venture outside.

Two blocks off the boardwalk the streets formed a black mirror, vast puddles reflecting the light from distant arcades. He walked across the veined parking lot and down an alley lined with popcorn-strewn trash cans, onto the wide wooden walkway where whispers would lead him along the beach to find the odd form that lay still in the sand.

He kept to himself as he went, avoiding eye contact with adults. Though tall for a nine-year-old, Bobby knew it was late for children to be roaming the boardwalk, and the last thing he wanted was to be dragged back and left alone with his mother after she woke up from one of her drunken comas.

A sudden outburst of laughter caused Bobby to pause at the edge of the alley. He observed a trio of sailors stumble past in uniform, two shoving the third ahead after a young woman who let out a mix of scream and giggle at their pursuit. Bobby liked her golden curls, how they bounced along her slender shoulders as she ran. Her smile, the way she glanced back like she was smiling at him, for him. Maybe this was how things were before the war, before his mother was left behind longing for someone to chase her.

And so Bobby raced after them, feet thumping against the wooden planks, imagining his hero, Ranger Bill, by his side. But they were too fast, the grown men swiping her off her feet and carrying her away before Bobby could catch his breath and cry for them to wait. In the dark at the edge of the boardwalk, the nearby screech of tires made him jump.

He looked toward the ocean, listening to the crash of the waves, the whispers of the sea breeze beckoning him closer. Memories of his father flickered through his head, first in hazy black and white like those in the family album, worn with ash and cigarette burns. Birthday parties and cookouts in the backyard, the smell of charcoal and the thick hair on his father's forearms as he flipped burgers in the sweltering heat. His pack of smokes kept tight in his rolled sleeve. Then came images he couldn't recall ever seeing before. Events layered in vibrant sepia so vivid it was like he was there in the moment. Being held in the hospital for the very first time, looking up at his father, teary eyed and unshaven. Running, tumbling around the backyard of the old house, his tiny feet catching on thick tree roots. Each thought interrupted by a flash, a camera capturing the scene.

Bobby longed for the summers when his father had let him stay up late, carrying him on his shoulders through the crowds, wind ruffling his hair, the smell of caramel corn tickling his nose. Those moments were more story than memory, but he had filled in the blanks and made them real. Taken the man he knew more from photographs and given him life after the war, after he went missing in some far off land beyond the sea.

He set one foot on the beach, then the other. The sand felt cool against his sun-burnt feet. He liked the zip noise his heels made as he shuffled toward the waves and the dark horizon. The sound of the surf grew with each step. And the memories—love, war, letters from overseas, men in uniform at his front door—came at such a furious pace he wrapped his hands around his head and squeezed until it hurt.

At once the images vanished, driven away by a pungent smell of brine and decay, like the time he dug up sand crabs, corralling them in a bucket under the hot sun. He looked down to see the strange creature at his feet, partially obscured under the torn red and white stripes of a windblown chair. The thing was dark blue, darker still in its crevices, slimy and covered with scales and spined ridges. Despite the waves lapping near its peculiar head, it lay face-down, motionless. Bobby toed the sand, uncovering a plastic shovel. Curious, he raised it and poked at the thing. The plastic clacked against its back, hard like an insect and unresponsive to touch.

But when he dragged the shovel down over its side, the tissue turned soft and the tip of the shovel slid into a tear where its stomach might reside, a deep cut that caused the creature to fidget.

Bobby's knees wobbled and he fell back on his rear, the tip of the shovel coated with a dark red stain. Warm visions returned, but of the sea and its sweet brine. The thing, grotesque now, turned its perverse head toward Bobby, chittering facial features disguised in sand. Its breath overwhelmed Bobby in a cloud of salt so thick it made him gag.

The whispers from the sea rose once more, this time in a peaceful chorus, calming Bobby's fears and giving strength to his limbs. He extended the shovel to the creature. It grabbed hold with a webbed paw, much like a toad, but with stubby digits. Bobby strained his back, pulling it with all his strength, out from under the chair toward the sea foam. It was smaller than he'd originally thought, much shorter than Bobby, but heavy, and when the creature kicked its short legs the chore became more difficult.

Finally, when Bobby was knee deep in the ocean the creature let go, engulfed in surf and rolled away with the tide, its skin blending with the brackish water.

Confused, Bobby dropped the shovel and started back for the motel. Only when he was halfway up the beach did he turn to see the glowing eyes hiding below the waves. And when the thing flipped and dove down, Bobby thought it might have waved goodbye.

What was that? Bobby shuddered. Like a spell had been broken, suddenly aware of how far out he'd ventured. The waves crashed against his backside, soaking the edge of his shirt as he waded back to shore. He could barely recall the previous moment, much less describe the creature in detail. But his chest tingled with excitement at the notion of the unknown, the sensation of an odd encounter that he'd never forget.

He picked over debris as he left, the usual clam and muscle shells dotting the shoreline. He spied an unfamiliar cone hiding amongst a bunch of yellow seaweed. Brushing the plant life aside, he dug his hands into the sand and pulled out a conch twice the size of a baseball. He held up the treasure in the soft moonlight, taking in the wonder of its blue-green ridges and natural curves like he was the luckiest boy on earth.

He floated to the motel, high on discovery, only realizing he'd reached his destination when he felt the cool metal door knob. The room appeared dark and quiet inside, the coin-op having run its course. When he opened the door to his mother's snoring, a sense of disappointment coursed through him, having to wait until the morning to share his find. He placed the treasure on the bedside table and slid under the covers. Soon his mother's snores became a heavy static, and he fell fast asleep, dreaming of a never-ending sea.

***

In the morning, Bobby laid in bed, slick with sweat, until sunlight pierced the shades and the heat woke his mother in a fit of coughing. He'd mulled the previous night's events for what felt like hours, unable to fully wrap his mind around them. It was too real to be a dream—damp sand was still stuck between his toes—but he couldn't fully recall his encounter with the strange creature, only snippets, like he'd seen it blurry from afar.

And the shell! How could he forget? But when he rolled to his side to admire the conch it was gone.

And his mother was screaming.

Bobby shot up straight in bed. Across the room his mother held her foot, dancing in pain.

"What the hell is this doing here?" She bent down and retrieved the conch from beside her bed, her face crimson with rage. "Bobby, what is this?" She didn't wait for an answer.

"No!" Bobby darted out of bed as she whipped open the door and hurled the mysterious shell into the parking lot. Bobby squeezed past, shoving her out of the way. The shell flew high, hurtling toward the pavement, shattering on impact.

"No, no, no." Tears welled in Bobby's eyes. He fell to his knees, cradling the broken pieces. Something moved within the mess; a crab-like crustacean, ugly and black as the tar-lined cement beneath it, struggled to move, impaled by a shard of its own shell.

"Ugh, Bobby, get away from that thing." His mother came up behind him, snatched hold of his hands and pulled him away.

"But Mom, I found it."

"Well you should have left it alone. Come inside and clean up. We're going to the beach."

* * *

Bobby trailed behind his mother, cooler chest and beach chairs adding to his burden as he dragged his feet, sulking with his head low.

"Keep it up and we're not going to get a good spot."

"Maybe you shouldn't sleep in so late," he muttered, a little too loud.

She paused, waiting for him to catch up. "What was that?"

"Nothing"

"That's what I thought. You watch it, young man. You're still on thin ice from this morning." His mother spun on her heels and continued toward the sea of umbrellas. Bobby always seemed to be tiptoeing on thin ice. He often wondered what it would take for him to fall through, and what would be waiting for him on the other side.

They settled on a spot close to the water, the hard packed sand still wet from the morning tide. Bobby helped spread out a towel in front of their chairs.

"Bobby, the oil." He rummaged through their bag for the baby oil. "And wipe your hands first, I don't want any sand mixed in."

Bobby disliked the greasy liquid, the way it crept under his fingernails and took forever to rub off. But he took his time rubbing it over her shoulders and back. If he missed a spot, he'd hear about it for days. After finishing with the oil he laid down on the towel, trying to relax. He hadn't slept well and a tired feeling crept into his eyes. They were always the first to feel it, and the strain from the sun didn't help.

But each time he was close to nodding off, his head began to hurt. A dull pain near the back of his skull throbbed with each wave as it crashed upon the shore, coming close to tickling his feet. Beneath the roar in his head, he heard a chittering sound like the clicking of teeth, faster and faster. And with each rush of water came painful memories of recent years spent alone with his mother. His inability to get anything right, the way she took her anger out on him when it was really meant for a co-worker or a bad date, the ashtrays and empty beer cans that dotted every surface of the apartment, the thin ice. The more he concentrated on falling asleep, the more the unhappiness intensified, until he felt like his head was going to explode. He flipped over and crawled on his hands and knees into the cold surf, rubbing his palms against the sandy bottom, clawing through loose shells until his limbs were numb and lobster red. He sat there letting the waves crash against him as bodies mingled in the shallows. A woman nearby shouted, "beer, beer!" and threw sea foam into the air, over the heads of splashing children. Twins body surfed past Bobby on either side, riding a small wave until they hit the beach.

A piece of torn fabric caught his attention, red and white stripes, stained with salt. It floated near Bobby, a slight dark bulge at its center. He shuddered, reaching toward the cloth, the chittering movements of the creature coming back to him. And as he touched the fabric, something dark burst from underneath. The spray blinded Bobby and he fell backward, his scream cut off as he went under, salt water filling his mouth and stinging his eyes. A strong hand pulled him up. An older kid with shaggy black hair and a dark blue wet suit asked if he was okay. Bobby stumbled away, collapsing on his towel, now dusted with sand from passerby, listening to his body throb in tune with the fast beat of his heart.

"There you are Bobby," his mother said. "I was beginning to wonder if you'd run off. Grab me a cold one from the cooler, would you?"

Face down, he rolled his eyes and waited until she called on him again.

***

The frustration grew by lunch, over newspaper-covered tables strewn with trays of steamed crabs.

"Stop that, Bobby, you're makin' a mess."

Bobby bounced a wooden mallet off the crab claw, its shell too thick to penetrate.

"Clean up and get your mother another beer."

"No."

"What do you mean, 'no'?"

Bobby answered with a repeated CRACK of the mallet, bringing it down on the crab claw again and again until it splintered and shell flew in every direction. His mother grabbed his wrist. Customers watched from nearby tables, whispering and frowning at the sight of the struggle.

"Stop that this instant!"

But he kept at it, overpowering her grip, making small semi-circular dents in the table.

"That's it, we're leaving." She ripped the mallet from his hand and yanked him from his chair. They marched the three blocks to the motel without exchanging a word.

"Sit on that bed and don't move a muscle until I return, you hear me?" She stabbed a finger at his chest. "I've had enough of your acting out."

She slammed the door. Bobby heard the click of the lock and the thwack of her flip-flops as she stormed off. He flopped back on the mattress, his limbs splayed out. Exhaled a long sigh, and by the time he realized the headache was gone, he fell fast asleep.

***

Later, Bobby lay awake, staring up at the ceiling from under the covers when the door swung open. His mother entered the room quietly, shrouded in darkness. She flicked on the light and sat down beside Bobby on the bed. He sat up against the headboard, rubbing his eyes. His mother's face looked like it had aged five years while she was away, her eyes and nose red from tears.

"I brought us some dinner." She crinkled a paper bag in her hands. It smelled of burgers and fries.

"Mama—"

"Shush, quiet now Bobby. I know it's been hard for us both since your father…. It's just sometimes I get so frustrated…" She quieted for a moment, rubbing an index finger across her lips before tilting her head back with an exhale, blinking tears away.

"I'm sorry, Bobby." She unrolled the bag and placed it on Bobby's lap. "Let's eat, okay?"

Bobby's mouth watered as the scent from the open bag filled the room. His mother circled to the other side of the small bed and squeezed under the covers next to Bobby. She took a couple fries from the bag and turned on the radio, cutting through static-tinged news until she found the program she was looking for, just in time for the intro to finish: Ranger Bill. Bobby's ears perked at the sound. It was an old episode, but one that he'd never heard before.

Bill, fresh off getting his pal Frenchy a new delivery job, gave commands to his crew as they set out to sea on a fishing trip.

"Steady now, men. We're heading to deep waters and there's no telling what we'll find. But I'll grant you this, we're not coming back until we've caught us each a fish!" A shout went up from the men and they went to work, readying the boat.

Bobby smiled as he munched on a greasy burger, no cheese, only ketchup; just the way he liked them. Ranger Bill always knew what to do. His mother put an arm around him, ran fingers through his hair and gave him a kiss on the forehead.

"Love you, kiddo."

They ate in silence and listened to the radio. When Bobby finished, he pulled the covers up to his chin and snuggled closer, tucking his head under her chin, the warmth of her chest against his cheek. He lived for these moments, as uncommon as they were.

"Goodnight," he said through a yawn, his eyes already closed.

***

Bobby dreamed that he was far out to sea on a ship lost in a storm while in search of sunken treasure. The wind howled and the sea sprayed his face, but he stood tall because Ranger Bill was there holding his hand.

"Steady now, Bobby!" he called, and together they braced for another wave. Bobby held on as it crashed over the boat. But when the water settled and he looked around, Bill was nowhere for be found.

"Bill," he cried. Another wave curled toward the boat. Bobby shrunk down, wrapping his arms around a column. And just as the wave crashed—SLAM—he shot awake.

***

Something was wrong.

He froze, still upright against the headboard. Darkness swallowed the motel room except for a tiny cone of light from an upended lamp in the corner. The radio buzzed with soft static. He shifted his weight, felt a damp sensation through the sheets. The bed was soaked. The smell... the familiar pungent stink of brine from the prior night. Bobby shivered, tried rubbing warmth into his arms.

"Mama?" He swung his feet to the side of the bed, stepped down into a warm puddle. He called out again, whispering this time, tip-toeing across the sodden carpet.

He cracked open the door, greeted by a cold breeze that almost made him jump. Outside, more puddles led away from the motel in the direction of the boardwalk. The cloudless sky was pitch black except for a sliver of moon. The streets were empty of life. No aura of neon descended from the boardwalk. No music, no laughter. Just the moon and its infinite-eyed smile. A slight shadow shifted near a broken street light, ducking low and disappearing, leaving behind a distinct click-click-click in its wake. That sound.

The haunting chittering of the creature repeated again and again in the distance. Bobby sprinted toward the boardwalk, jumping over garbage cans that had been dented and knocked over, spilling their contents down the alleyway.

He saw them from the boardwalk.

Them.

Several of the strange things bobbed in the ocean, something large filled the space between them, just beneath the surface.

"Mama!" He screamed as he sprinted across the sand, alongside a shallow depression which disappeared with the high tide. The tiny heads turned back to him eyes ablaze, and melted beneath the waves.

Bobby collapsed at the edge of the tide, head wracked with mingling flashbacks of the past. He wept; howled tormented cries for the sea to spit back his mother and father and make them whole again. And in the midst of the storm of memories, he heard a voice.

Steady now, men. We're heading to deep waters and there's no telling what we'll find.

Bobby stood up tall, shaking with nervous energy, but his legs wouldn't budge. His despairing hands hung empty at his sides while the hungry waves buried his feet beneath the sand.

Safe Inside the Violence

THE house on Chappie looks the same as it did thirty years ago when my mother threw in the towel and dragged me across the river to live with her sister in Revere. An old man in baggy sweats sits on the adjacent concrete stoop. Clear plastic tubing pulls oxygen up through his nose from a small canister beside him. A nub of cigar hovers over the sidewalk between his fingers. He's kept an eye on me through his Coke-bottle lenses since I set foot on the block. Same old townies. I'm fitting the key in the deadbolt lock when I hear him spit.

"Your father was a pain in my ass," he says, loud enough to know it's meant for me. I leave the key in the door, lean back to get a better look. "Kelly, right?" He yanks the tubing free from his nose, bites down on the remnants of the cigar with crooked ash-colored teeth.

"Tommy," I say, confirming more than I want to give him.

He introduces himself as Sean, tells me, "You look just like him."

"He owes me twenty bucks for kicking first. I'll let it slide. I bet on myself to go first too." The joke brings about an awful wheeze-fueled chuckle that sees him struggling to reinsert the tubing. He jabs a cheek and the side of his nose before getting it on the third try. I'm preparing myself to watch him die right there on the steps, another relic of the old days up in smoke. The veins crisscrossing the backs of his hands protrude like bones. He grips the tops of his knees and hunches over. Oxygen hisses as it whooshes into his system. I unlock the door and tell him I'll see him around. He looks up to say goodbye, but it's clear he's not ready yet.

My father left me his three-bedroom brick townhouse in Charlestown, a 2002 Chevy Malibu with more miles than I'd ever seen put on a car, twenty thousand dollars, and a leather-bound journal which I tossed, unread, into the trash outside the Dunkin' Donuts on Main.

His attorney agreed to meet me for coffee. He spent the fifteen minutes attempting small talk, none of which I wanted. Neither did the regulars around us. The funeral was nice, turnout was as expected. Not a lot of friends, but the ones he had were good ones as they say. It's a New England thing. I left him having signed the paperwork, initialed here and there, answering only one of his questions—I hadn't seen my father in twenty five years and no, it doesn't bother me.

The air inside is thick with spice. My father sublet the spare bedrooms to foreign students for extra cash. They pay on time and mind their own business. One from China, the other from Pakistan, though they'd change every six months to a year or so.

It's warm for December. I open a couple of windows

to air the place out, grab a beer from the fridge and collapse on the couch. The rest of the house can wait. I channel surf through news. The Bruins don't skate for another hour.

I'm asleep when the kids get home. One of them shouts at me from the kitchen, the other holds a steak knife. They look like they've encountered a stranger sleeping on the couch before, or maybe they left me sleeping while they over-thought their plan of attack. Either way, it takes longer than it should to calm them down. The Chinese, Arthur, the Pakistani, Josh—Anglo names they've chosen to represent them while in the States—make introductions and apologize. I tell them not to worry, it's all new to me too, and offer them a hundred dollars each to clear out my dad's stuff. They practically leap at the money. An hour later I find six trash bags out back on the brick patio. Except for three bare trees that anchor the far end, the narrow yard is free of leaves and debris. A short chain-link fence marks the perimeter, with a gate to the alley that separates the building from the old man's place. Shadows quickly descend over the neighborhood, and I'm reminded of how cold winter can be. What had been some kind of light fixture hangs cockeyed over the neighbor's back door, bulb shattered, filament exposed to the wind. A coffee can overflows with cigarette butts to the side, below the broken light. The patio is covered in charcoal dust from an overturned grill. A privacy fence could have saved a lot of heartache around here. I turn in before the sight depresses me further.

I carry my suitcase upstairs. A storage unit containing

the remainder of my belongings rides on the back of a semi somewhere west of the Mississippi. LA's a long way from Boston. My receipt reads an optimistic two weeks until delivery.

Josh is in my old room with the door closed. I imagine the four walls, twin bed, closet—always closed—within. I let him have his privacy. It's not something I especially need to see.

True to the evidence outside, the pair didn't shy away from their assignment. I wonder if they found it cathartic, tossing everything their landlord left behind. When I close the door an aluminum bat clatters to the hardwood floor. The sound makes me jump. A brief thought flashes through my head—that this is *my* bat—but that can't be true. Everything had been borrowed, down to the oversized glove. I shut the closet door, set my suitcase beside his—*the* desk—and flop onto the mattress. They stripped the sheets and pillow cases too.

I concentrate on my toes, instruct them to go to sleep, fade away. By the time I reach my knees, the jet lag hits and I'm out.

***

Sometime later I open my eyes in the dark room. Arthur pokes me in the face with an index finger. "Wake up, Mr. Kelly," he says.

I tell him, "It's Tommy," and lay there listening to bass thud against the house. Sean's throwing quite a party. Arthur needs sleep, says he's a morning person. That's when he gets his best work done. I roll off the mattress and peek through the blinds. Every light in the house is on; silhouettes lurk behind the pulled shades. I ask Arthur if he called the cops. He says no, as if the thought never occurred to him. I tell Arthur to sit tight, and head outside. The temperature has plummeted since the afternoon. I ring Sean's doorbell three times, stand shivering on the stoop as wind whips into the alcove. Another round of rings and I hear footsteps. Multiple locks ratchet, the door swings wide revealing a younger, stouter version of Sean. My stomach recoils at the stench of bad weed that bursts from within. He looks past me, out into the night, as if I might be some kind of lure.

"What?" he says, stepping forward. I can smell the whiskey on his breath. "You look familiar."

"I'm your neighbor."

"Oh," he says, taking a minute to process the words. "We're celebrating."

"That's nice. Can you tone it down?"

"My brother just got out of jail." When I hesitate, he says, "Three years."

"That's nice." I mention time off for good behavior. The idea makes him laugh, as if his brother would rather die in prison before toeing the line.

He cranes his neck back inside, voice booming, "Hey, Dougie!" then waves off the idea. "Nah, he's busy. You want a beer?"

"Where's your old man?"

"He's lying down. Can't hold his liquor nowadays."

I take a deep breath. The need to be here, right here, in this moment disgusts me. I walk away before I say something stupid. The door slams shut behind me, the party rolls on.

Upstairs in the hallway, the floorboards creaking beneath my feet, Arthur cracks open his door. I tell him that I've taken care of it. He dips his head, thanks me profusely and slips away. Back on the mattress, my cell phone lays on my chest, fingers hover over it to dial the cops. Scenarios play out all jumbled together in my head. None of them seem worth the effort. I close my eyes and hope for the best.

***

The house is quiet when I wake. It's late morning, the students are gone. The kitchen smells of coffee and cinnamon. Dirty dishes fill the sink. The coffee maker is turned on though its light is off, timed out. I unplug it from the wall and warm up the dregs in a beige mug. It tastes cheap and bitter. My last sip is full of grounds.

I pull on a beige souvenir hoodie, SANTA MONICA across the chest in bold script, complete with a cigarette burn on the right sleeve. The Malibu is parked out front on the street. I find keys in an envelope in the package from the attorney.

He's waiting for me, parked his ass on the hood, a wad of gum packed in his cheek. I take him to be Dougie, the newly freed man, his features an uncanny mix of father and brother. He could be a year older than his brother, or ten. We lock eyes as I descend the steps, walk around the rear of the car, postponing the inevitable.

"You mind?" I slot the key in the driver's side door, twist to unlock. He slides the wad of gum from one cheek to the other, hocks it into the street.

"Heard you stopped by last night."

"That's right." I open the door, hold it in front of me like a shield.

"Call the cops?"

"No."

"But you were thinking about it, weren't you?" He smiles. Three top teeth are missing on the left side. I can see his tongue flick against his molars. "Yeah, I know your type." He points to his head. "Thinkers."

I feel my face growing hot, get the feeling he can sense it too. I climb inside and shut the door. Through the windshield I tell him to move, that I'm not going to ask again. When he calls my bluff, staring me down with hardened eyes, I put the key in the ignition and turn. The dials across the dash flip back and forth to a series of clicks and whirrs. Battery's shot. I try again, and again, on autopilot in disbelief. The car's shocks squeal as he stands. He knocks on the window. I open the door into him, forcing him back to give me space.

"Whoa there," he says, hands up, innocent. "Need a jump?"

A *fuck you* lodges in my throat. I lock up and slam the door shut.

"Not very neighborly," he calls after me as I storm off. I don't wait to hear the rest.

***

It takes blocks for me to calm down, to slow my pace. A maddened cowardice clings to my shoulders like a parasite, furious at my decision to come home—to even think of it as that word—*home*. I grab a bite at a pizza joint, order an extra slice to go. The cable's out when I return, even the local channels read 'unavailable'. I sit on hold for thirty minutes to learn they'll send a truck out to take a look. Maybe today, probably tomorrow.

At night I chase sleep, raking my nails over the mattress in frustration. It's nearly midnight when I hear the neighbor's screen door squeak open and slap shut. I'm out of bed, kneeling at the window by the third time. The younger brother drags his feet down the alley to a car idling in front of the house. He gets in for no more than a minute, enough for a brief conversation, and then it's out and back down the alley, a wad of cash in hand. The deal is so brazen, it's stupid. I'm overly curious, glued to the window waiting for his next trip. It takes minutes. But this time it's Dougie who pokes his head out. When he looks up at my window, I fall back onto my heels, cocooned panic fluttering in my chest. The room is dark, he can't possibly see me, and yet his focus stays on the house. Worse, when he reaches the front, there's no customer. I return to the mattress bearing a sense of defeat, unsure of what I've lost. The moon cuts through the blinds in slivers, forming a cage around the bed. I curse myself, and spend the rest of the night tossing and turning.

Come morning, I have to get out of the house. A cable technician finds wires ripped out of the cable box on the side of the building, and the storage unit has arrived much earlier than expected. The driver looks asleep on his feet, his movements in slow motion. I sign all of the paperwork without reading a word, anything to make him go away. There's a liquor store two blocks west. I'm not picky, Jameson's acceptable. The guy ringing me up wears a mask of no emotion. He takes my crumpled bills and wraps the fifth in a paper bag. I uncap it and take a pull in the doorway. He doesn't seem to mind that either, so I take another. I'm half in the bag by the time I set foot on my block. The sight makes my heart shrivel, numb itself to sleep. The storage locker has been ripped open, my life spilled over the street and nearby cars. I set the bottle on the step, pick up the scraps one by one and place them back in the unit. Not a word escapes my lips as I work. The clothes are covered in sand and salt, books and small furniture torn and smashed. I find the broken lock—it's been cut—and slip it through the opening to hold the clasp shut. I'm sure I missed something, but I no longer possess the energy to look. I don't bother calling the cops. If they didn't come for my mother, they won't come for me.

In the kitchen I take one last pull and whip the bottle against the wall. It smashes into a thousand pieces, whiskey sprays in a wide arc. My ears flood with imagined screams. I leave a note on the counter, scribble CLEAN IT in all caps, then go back and add PLEASE, with another pair of one hundred dollar bills.

I steal a beer from the fridge and head upstairs. I sit in a corner of my room nursing the bottle, the aluminum bat resting at my feet. The wall is cold against my back. Radiators knock and hiss, compensating for the lack of insulation. I hear ghostly whispers of my parents fighting, slamming doors. My mother sobs into her pillow at the foot of my bed. Violence pumps through my bloodstream with every thud of my heart. I feel the tourniquet slipping.

Cloud cover shuts out the moon. I can barely see my hands, let alone which of the brothers passes within feet of me, wandering down the alley for their nightly gig. In the end it doesn't matter. I unhinge the gate, slip through and move across their back patio.

His return is on cue. I sneak up behind, follow him inside. It's the younger of the two. He calls out to his brother, "Hey Dougie," as we pass through the laundry room, into the kitchen. It reeks of weed and smoke and something else—something rotten. Suddenly he stops, as if he can smell it too. Before he can turn I swing low. His right knee explodes, buckling inward. He cries out falling, reaching for his leg, and I kick him in the face, right in the mouth. Dougie hurtles into view swearing death. I swing as he rushes me, hear his left forearm snap, and then I'm flying backward into the counter. My head snaps into a cabinet. He drills me in the stomach with his good hand before I can recover. I lose my grip on the bat, hear it bounce against the floor as my vision blurs. He grabs a fistful of my hoodie, shoots his head forward connecting with my cheek. Pain flares across my face. I panic, blindly swipe an arm across the counter searching for anything. My fingers find glass. He rears his head back and I meet it with a liquor bottle. The sound of it against his skull makes me sick. He collapses in a heap, his legs contort at awful angles. White-knuckled, I clutch the unbroken bottle. My head is spinning, limbs shaking with adrenaline. It hurts to breathe.

The rotten smell reasserts itself, drawing me across the kitchen to a door that opens inward to the basement. I flick the switch on the wall. The entry remains dark. A dim light glows from the unseen bottom. The staircase is rotten, wood bending under the weight of my steps. The basement is no better, crowded with clutter. A path has been cleared, leading to a blue tarp shoved against the back wall. Sean's oxygen canister resting atop a stack of old windows tells me all I need to know, but I pull back the tarp and look anyway, see his head loll at an unnatural angle atop a pale neck ringed with bruises. I've seen enough.

The brothers are still down. I swipe a flip phone from the counter next to a pile of uncashed disability checks, tell the police of the body. I leave the bottle in the sink, take the bat and the phone with me, and toss the phone in the trash outside.

I fill a plastic bag with ice, press it against my face to slow the swelling. I take the steps upstairs one a time, a hand on the wall keeping me steady. In my room I pull open the dresser drawers one by one. Soon blue lights tease against the window. I crack the blinds to let them in, let them dance on the walls as I empty my suitcase in my new home.

Napoleon of the
North End

THE small package was too carefully wrapped for Ornello to ignore, and so before the hydraulic press could drag it under, he reached a hand in and plucked it from the maw of the garbage truck. The black plastic covering stunk of rotten vegetables and spoiled meat, like everything else in the North End of Boston on trash day. He'd gotten used to the smell over his first year on the job—so much so that after wiping a layer of slime from the bag against his thigh, he unzipped the top of his Carhartt jacket and stuffed the package inside, tight against his chest. Opening himself up to the wind off the sea felt like dumping ice down his shirt. Still, his cheeks blushed and his scalp underneath his hat dampened with sweat at the thought of the object.

The March air was bitter cold, city streets decorated with gray icebergs of melting snow that made it difficult for the truck to maneuver around cars parked at odd angles. He held tight to the grip on the back of the truck, snapping a thumb against the metal while the hydraulic system compacted the block's waste. Loud and painfully slow, the whine finally cut off, replaced by the rumble of the diesel engine and a thick cloud of exhaust beneath Ornello's feet as he stepped onto the back. Carmine took them through a tight intersection with a wide turn that missed a light pole by less than a foot, jumped the sidewalk and reversed down a cobblestone alley. His thirty years of experience at the wheel made driving half-blind and hung-over look easy.

Only then in the alley did Ornello relax. The North End housed an alarming number of retired full-blooded Italians—including his grandparents—with nothing to do except sip espresso, read the paper, and watch the happenings on the street below from their high-rise apartments. Heckling from the old-timers was a daily occurrence. Fluency had stopped in his family with his father's generation, but Ornello understood enough to know his reputation as a fuck-up had made the rounds. From day one, after his father pulled strings to land him the gig, they'd watched for him. Given a play-by-play of trash bags that ripped as he tossed them toward the truck, showering the street in filth. The embarrassment of losing his breakfast in the aftermath. For a week he tried giving it back to them, slamming their trash cans until they cracked and tossing their lids into the compactor.

Until his father caught wind.

And true to his old man's reputation as a delegator, Carmine sent Ornello home nursing a black eye and busted lip. Carmine, pissed off in his own right at Ornello for making the truck look bad and bringing heat on them both. For a guy pushing sixty he sure could throw a punch.

Ornello had shrugged off the lesson on neighborhood justice, but memories of the events afterward made his heart race against the package snug against his chest.

The dumpster in the alley was full as usual, but Ornello got through the bags in half the time, eager for a peek at his prize. At last he slapped the red button to compact and pulled out the package. It had a weight to it, heavier than before when he'd rescued it from the truck. The black plastic bag was tied closed with tight knots, so he ripped into the side to find a stained gray shirt, balled up and smelling of oil and something else. He pinned his right hand in his armpit and tugged off his thick glove. Gently pried away the folded layers, avoiding the curious blotches of dark red, until the dim light in the alley caught on the cylinder of a revolver. The whine of the compactor stalled, and without thinking Ornello slapped the button down again to buy more time. He spread away more of the shirt to get a full look at the pistol. It was small, no bigger than his hand, with a stubby barrel like the tip had been sawed off. The cylinder, by comparison, was large, almost disproportionally so. He held it gently, caressed it from nose to grip with more care than he'd given his newborn nephew.

A blast of the truck's horn gave him a start and he dropped the bundle. He clapped his hands together to catch it at his waist before it hit the alley floor. Tossed the ripped plastic to the ground and stuffed the hurriedly wrapped bundle back inside his jacket. It didn't look as good as when he'd first found it, but it would do. He slipped his glove on and hopped on the side as Carmine began to pull away without him. Wind whipped down the street stinging, his eyes as they made the turn, but at his core he felt a warmth he'd been missing.

Home was a few blocks off Hanover Avenue, nestled in the middle of the North End. A studio the size of a large walk-in closet, the steep price kept him and Flora together more than anything else. The strong, stubborn Italian blood that ran deep in them both made for a rare day without a scuffle over something they knew ultimately meant little to either of them. But the heartache was worth it, as his Grandma Noni made a point to remind him every other Sunday during family dinners. Once you've got a hold on a bella ragazza you don't let her out of your sight. The struggle is good for the soul, she'd say and thump her chest with a gnarled fist.

"Yo, Flora, I'm home," he called as he turned his key, opening the door. Inside the quiet apartment, a note on the fridge explained she'd gone in early to cover for a waitress who left sick—or pregnant, he could hear her say. She'd developed a habit of adding the phrase after everything. Not coming out for drinks? Waddaya, pregnant? Quit whining, you're acting like you're pregnant. It started when her sister announced she was carrying the family's first grandchild and permanently vacuumed the attention from the room. Bets had been lost on when it would stop. He left the note beneath the photo magnet of the two of them at a wedding last fall. It was a silly shot—decked out in photo booth gear, large sunglasses and funny hats—but her personality leapt from the picture. Her long hair was pulled back in the photo revealing the olive skin of her neck. The slight cleavage formed by the tight dress taunted him. He let out an audible sigh. Such is the life of opposite schedules. A vacation was overdue.

Despite the odor that clung to him, he took advantage of

her absence and postponed the usual order of immediate shower. Kicked off his boots and carried the bundle to the table, laying it beside a polished antique lamp. He considered the lamp to be one of his prized trophies from the job. He'd discovered it shortly after knocking heads with Carmine. A treasure merely in need of a good spit shine, left out between two trash bags on a rainy day. Despite the reprimands and the still swollen eye, he'd kept it, held it under his arm as the truck pulled away. Within seconds an elderly man had appeared on the sidewalk clutching a baseball bat thicker than his biceps. He'd chased after the truck at a slow jog, full of threats and curses. Ornello had frozen to the truck in shock at the sight, anxious for the inevitable next stop. The truck made a turn, stopping less than a car-length around the side of the building. He waited for the old man to show, but he never did. Thought about poking his head out and peering around the corner to make sure he didn't drop dead in the street. But they were falling behind schedule. Never did see him again, but the lamp sure was a nice touch to the apartment. Flora even approved of the addition for a change.

He clicked on the lamp and repeated the process of unwrapping the revolver, though this time with the realization the stains were definitely blood. He disregarded the crimson mystery and lifted the gun, rotating it in his hand. He'd never handled one before, but he'd seen enough movies to know not to point the gun at himself, and to keep his finger away from the trigger. Tried spinning the cylinder and found it locked in place. After a bit of finagling he popped it open to find three rounds still chambered, 38 SPL stamped into the rear of the bullet's casing. It smelled of smoke, and the insides of the empty chambers were dusted with gray flecks. He rotated the cylinder with his fingers to get a feel of it, then spun it against his palm and snapped it into place like he'd seen on television. It wasn't a Glock like they carried on all the cop shows, but it was pretty damn cool. He tossed the bloodied shirt in the garbage can underneath the sink and carried the pistol to his dresser, where he swaddled it in a ratty Red Sox t-shirt from the 2004 World Series and stuffed it beneath a stack of clothing in the bottom drawer.

Snatched a Narragansett tallboy from the fridge. The Red Sox were finishing up their pre-season in Florida, beating up on a squad of Blue Jays already reduced to another "rebuilding year." Turned the volume up so he could hear the game in the shower and carried the beer to the bathroom. If he spent another minute stinking up the tiny place, he knew Flora would let him hear about it when she got home. With her skin and hair thick with the smell of marinara and fried ravioli, though, he thought she might as well have been out with the truck all day. He'd said as much once and paid for it. He took a deep gulp of lager and let the hot water scald his skin.

Carmine splayed a copy of the morning's Boston Globe across the small table at Dunks and took a sip of his coffee—regular, extra, extra sugar. All part of their early morning ritual. Ornello leaned back in his chair, bored. He'd caught the ball game and the post analysis, which left him with little to check on his phone. Celtics were a disaster, Bruins were on a hot streak per usual, and another five months until the Pats took the field. If it wasn't sports it wasn't news. He took a sip of too-sweet coffee—Carmine only ordered his way, but hell, he was buying—and cleared his throat to get the older man's attention. When he cleared his throat for a second time, the man's eyes briefly flicked up, then back to the paper.

"What? Can't you see I'm reading here?"

"Itching to get goin'. Why don't we knock it out early?"

"Because then we'd have nothing to do at the end of the day."

"Plenty of things to do."

"Like what? Watch a game and jack off?" Carmine took another sip. "There are things you can learn from the paper, you know. You should educate yourself, be a good citizen in your community."

"I am a good citizen. I take out the trash."

"Not this kind of trash," said Carmine, tapping an article on the back of the front page. "Looks like the cops only got one of 'em."

"One of what?"

"Those creepers prowling the streets of the North End, you dunce."

"Oh, that weirdo who's been groping chicks or something?"

Carmine laid the paper down. "Groping chicks? We got a rapist on the loose in our backyard and all you got is 'groping chicks'? This brain of mine might be running half-speed, but if I remember correctly you got a lady friend working nights out there. Might want to give that some thought. Capisce?"

Ornello waved off the older man's advice. Looked out the window while drinking his coffee to fill the silence and hide his shame. Little made him angrier than an attack on his pride. But the coffee shop was mostly empty, the few around them minding their own business, and so he swallowed his wounds with the last of the syrupy coffee.

"You know, this shit is disgusting."

Carmine didn't bother looking up. "Don't like it? Buy your own."

Ornello shrugged, grinned over a tight jaw. The man was right.

Carmine's mention of the rapist stuck with Ornello as they made their rounds through Back Bay, haunting his every move. Did he know the man? Had he seen him on the streets? Police could say little about the suspect. He was a white male with dark, short hair and tall, maybe six feet—a general enough description that fit too many to count, including him. Could Flora be in real danger? He felt like an asshole for disregarding her safety. Couldn't wait to get back to the North End to do his part, be more vigilant. He wouldn't allow her to walk to and from the restaurant alone. Couldn't trust any of those wimps working alongside her to protect her. Didn't want them getting any bright ideas either, thinking they could muscle in on him. No, Ornello had to be in charge. He tossed another pair of bags in the compactor, glass shattering as he whipped them inside. The end of his route couldn't come soon enough.

Ornello tore the note from the fridge, crumpled it in his

palm and pitched it into the sink. Another early shift. Sorry xoxo. The release he'd been waiting for all day ballooned like a gas in his belly. Meeting her at the restaurant on a Friday night was off the table. Too many customers, and the stress would only cause a scene. He ripped open the fridge, cracked a fresh tallboy and sucked half of it down. Let out a deep belch that helped calm his nerves. Still, his stomach felt uneasy, his body tense. He set the beer on the table, stepped to the dresser and opened the drawer, fishing for the gun. Felt a moment of panic when his fingers came up empty, and then realized he must have shoved it further back in the drawer. He pulled it out by a corner of the t-shirt, unwrapped it on the floor and carried it to the table with both hands. The revolver looked good next to the lamp. Not perfect—it could use a stand of some kind to show it off, but it looked like it belonged. He finished the beer while admiring his newest treasure. Snagged another and headed for the shower.

He toweled off in front of the bathroom mirror. Struck a magazine cover pose, flexing his chest and biceps. Looked pretty damn good for a guy who hauled shit around all day.

Flora wasn't big on surprises, but he planned to wait for her outside the restaurant when her shift ended around one. Hell, maybe he'd even bring her flowers. Really pour on the knight in shining armor shtick.

He slapped some cologne on his neck and chest and picked out a nice sweater and a clean pair of jeans. All he had to do was wait. No Sox, but the Bruins would do— home against the Blue Jackets, guaranteed entertainment. He set two beers out on the coffee table and put a bowl of Flora's leftover pasta in the microwave. A horn blared on the television; the Bruins scoring their first goal less than a minute into the game. He smiled. It was going to be a good night.

He woke groggy, mouth tasting of sleep and flat beer. Shot upright when he recognized the late night talking heads on the screen. Rubbed his eyes and cursed himself and the six-pack of empties on the table. The clock on the wall read ten minutes till one. Just enough time for him to make it to the restaurant. He ran to the bathroom and gargled mouthwash while taking a quick piss. Threw on his coat, but slowed as he crossed the room, running a hand along the table, the revolver inches from his fingers. He'd been so focused on Flora walking home that he'd almost forgotten about the gun.

He picked it up, wrapping his right hand around the grip, weighing it in his hand. It felt good, secure. He slotted it in the right hand pocket of his coat. A quick glance in the mirror and he was out the door.

"What do you mean she took off early?" Ornello said to the manager. He stood outside in the cold, the gut of the older man wedged in the doorway, blocking Ornello's path.

"Well, not really early I suppose. Just a few minutes ago. I let her go since the crowd had wound down."

"Thanks a lot, pal. Bunch of creeps prowling the street and you just let her walk off." He stabbed a finger in the man's direction and turned to leave. The man called after him, but Ornello was already across the street, hustling back to the apartment.

How could he have missed her? He'd been vigilant, looking at every face he passed, especially the men, committing them to memory should the need arise. He retraced his steps, leaving the last of the late-nighters on Hanover. He stuffed his hands in his coat pockets, clutched the cold metal. His gut felt off—something was wrong.

A sudden yelp stopped him in his tracks, tensed his muscles in a quick, painless spasm. From up ahead in a shadowed alcove came a deep chuckle of bass—a man's voice—followed by another high-pitched yelp, cut off and muffled to a moan.

Ornello crept in a wide angle around the corner. The scene slammed into him in slow motion, almost causing him to trip over his own feet.

"Hey!" he yelled.

A woman—Flora—ripped herself from the man's grasp.

"Oh my god, Ornello!" she screamed as she pushed off the man, throwing him further into the shadows, and ran away in the direction of their apartment.

"What the hell was that?" said the man, stepping into the light. White male, short dark hair… before he could take more than two steps, Ornello was on him, slamming him into the brick wall.

"Teach you to—" Ornello managed to get out before the man caught him in the throat with a forearm, shoving him back into a parked car.

"Fuck off, kid," he said, hocking spit across the brick sidewalk as Ornello coughed, grasping at his bruised throat. The man adjusted his tie, turned in the direction Flora had fled. Ornello lunged for him, fingers snagging the back of his collar. Ornello fumbled for the pistol in his jacket. The man spun to face him as he pulled it loose, finger on the trigger.

CLICK.

The man's forehead smashed into the bridge of Ornello's nose. His vision blurred. Finger still on the trigger.

BOOM.

The concussive blast forced hot air against his chest and face. The sound deafening, and yet so far away. The man fell against him, leaking warmth like smoke from his chest. Ornello staggered back in shock. He watched the man as he fell still then looked down at gun in his hand. Nearby trash cans seemed to glow with purpose.

Trash cans. He grabbed a lid—think, damn it, too close to the scene. Ran to the end of the block, cut right then left. Ripped the top off a plastic can and slipped the gun beside a foul mix of small bags repurposed for trash. Covered the can and sprinted home in a daze. When he slammed the door and slumped down against it, he recalled nothing from the trip. There was no sign of Flora, her phone rang straight to voice-mail. Unable to see straight, he fell asleep to the sound of sirens.

The morning smell of garbage was almost sweet. He hadn't been able to eat anything, nor drink the coffee that turned cold in his hand. Flora hadn't shown up, but he knew he had to get out of the apartment and go about his day. He stared out the window of the coffee shop, trying to ignore Carmine as he read aloud the details of the murder of a wealthy accountant gunned down in the North End. "Creepers one day, murderers the next. What is this world coming to? In my day, we took care of our own. Not like you kids."

His hand hurt from holding tight to the side of the truck. Tried to calm his anxiety by working the route slow and methodical, but the pace picked up with each block, waiting to round the corner and reach the cans that held his secret.

Finally, late in the morning, Carmine hit the brakes, dropping Ornello beside the dreaded cans. Slowly, unable to control his shaking limbs, he stepped from the truck. Recognized the guilty party, separate from the other two. Tossed those in first before returning to the third. Held his breath as he removed the lid. Let it dangle from his fingertips as he stared into the can at the cluster of small bags, the crevice where he had tucked the gun. Dragged the can to the truck, angled it into the compactor and watched for the revolver as each bag toppled into the trash heap. One by one they fell without a hint of the weapon until there were none left. He shook the can to be sure. Stuck a hand inside, groping around the cylinder. His body broke out in a sweat.

He threw the can toward the sidewalk, toppling its cousins. Tore into the bags in the back of the truck, opening one after the other. Spilled orange peels, spoiled meat covered in maggots and chunks of something green all over and into the street. Felt the eyes of the city fall on him, staring into his soul, tearing at his guilty conscious. Fast and faster he tore, finding nothing again and again until the blare of the horn made him jump, jolting him from his frantic searching. He straightened and looked from window to window, to shop fronts and passersby. No one giving him a second of their day. He was invisible.

Impatient, Carmine sounded the horn again. Ornello slapped the compact button and held on as they pulled away, watching trash disappear beneath the stained metal.

Blind Spot

THE whole thing reeked of some backwater porno shoot. Between the intense humidity and a trashcan full of black banana peels leftover by some previous knucklehead, each breath felt like inhaling a cloud of thick custard. Jim stood with his arms crossed, more wrinkles in his suit than his fifty-year-old face, wishing he'd brought a second six-pack along for the show. The quality of the video feed was acceptable, but the awkward angle of the hidden camera made him feel detached from the deal, as if he was miles away, unable to clearly see the person in the adjacent motel room.

"She's something, ain't she?" Rob said. Typical first words out of a rookie's mouth. Jim ignored him, sucked on a handful of mints he hoped would calm the hops that still danced on his tongue. He checked his watch, listening to the second hand clicking around the dial. It had taken longer than usual to get in touch with Sherri. He should already be home, asleep on the couch. Delila, his cranky old mutt, would protest when he eventually slid his fat ass alongside her. It had become an uncomfortable nightly ritual in the past week.

"Cleaning lady must have bumped the lamp." Rob took a swig of cold coffee, nodding toward the monitor. The camera had been turned so the agents could only see the back half of the room. The entryway was a blind spot. Jim watched Sherri as she returned from double-checking the door locks, pacing back and forth, hands fidgeting for the cigarettes he'd promised her as a reward for showing up on such short notice. She paused in front of the bed, tying back her dyed-blond hair in a short ponytail, arched back lifting her breasts underneath a tight white spaghetti-strap tank top. His favorite color. Jim ran a hand across his goatee. She'd dressed for him, even polished her nails a deep red. His eyes drifted to her slender neck, the purple Rorschach birthmark on her left shoulder blade. He stuffed his hands in his pockets and took a seat across the room from Rob. The drinks sloshed in his belly. He should've had something to eat.

"We should correct it, right? What if she makes the deal in the doorway?"

Sure kid. "Whatever you want to do."

"You tell me. She was already in the room when I got here." Rob stood and stripped off his new University of Florida sweatshirt, exposing muscled abs and his pistol secured in a shiny paddle holster. Fresh out of the academy and ready to take on the world like a regular Captain America. Back in the day, Jim parked senior agents' cars outside the New York City field office for the first three months of his career. When he finally got on a squad, he was handed twelve cold cases, an '85 Taurus (crippled survivor of four accidents) and kicked out the door. If you're at your desk, you're not working. Hit the streets.

Times had changed, and the new crop was a bunch of self-entitled pussies. Jim couldn't stand the rookie, but Rob was the only one on the squad without a family, who wouldn't bitch if he got called in after hours for the third time in a week. That, and he wouldn't ask questions. Not the kind of questions that mattered, at least. All the kid wanted to do was work, and Jim had more than enough to spread around.

"So, what's the story? Why the late drug buy?"

Jim raised a finger to his lips. "Nothing but air between these walls. Keep talking and we'll find ourselves in shit quick."

Rob shrugged, lowered his voice to just above a whisper. "What if you give her a quick ring? Ask her to move it?"

Jim ignored him and checked his watch again. He was done taking advice, especially the constant, unsolicited banter that spewed from the mouths of new agent babies. Their need to share the latest tactics, correct the old timers' aim at the range. Theirs was always a faster, better way of doing things. But Jim's methods were tried and true. Twenty years on the job—he'd earned it. Knew the shortcuts, knew when to stick his neck out (rarely), when to keep his mouth shut (most of the time). And you never volunteered without knowing exactly what you were signing up for. A week spent in a freezing warehouse "guarding" a confiscated yacht before it could be moved to a secure location had put an end to that. It was an important lesson Rob had yet to learn.

Jim's time with the FBI wasn't perfect, but no one made it through their career without a couple of internal investigations and a few days on the bricks with an unpaid vacation. If you weren't being looked at, you weren't doing your job.

Sherri bent down to smooth out the cheap comforter, a red thong that matched her nails briefly exposed by her low-cut jeans...and which also matched the one Jim's wife had found balled in the pocket of his slacks. He'd nearly fainted when she confronted him at dinner. For the first time in his life he was choked for words, GUILTY written on his stunned forehead. A meatball had slipped off his fork onto his plate, splattering red sauce across his dress shirt. He'd nervously dabbed at it with a napkin as he stumbled through his explanation, damning Sherri in one breath as some useless throwaway whore whom he'd worked with on a drug case for the past month, then praising himself in the next for helping her kick her heroin addiction. The jumbled mess of truths and lies was written in the red splotches all over his neck and face.

Rob let out a low, airy whistle. "Where'd you find her?"

Jim didn't answer. He was still thinking about his wife and her increasingly vocal threats to ruin him. A messy divorce was one thing—he'd closed down many a bar with friends and coworkers over the years who were going through a similar situation—but destroying his career was another. One phone call to the local papers and he'd have a gaggle of reporters up his ass until he retired, or was forced out. In a field where all you had to live by was your reputation, he was way past flirting with disaster.

Sherri stretched across the bed, the muscles in her arms and back flexed taught as she limbered up. *Probably going for a run after this. Or prepping to drag me into her room and tear my clothes off. Wouldn't that be nice to catch on camera? FBI agent fucks source in motel after drug buy. Film at eleven.*

"No wonder I can't get your attention." Rob relaxed back into a chair and kicked his feet up on a side table. "Where can I get a source like her?"

"Keep your dick in your pants. It's...something I taught her."

Rob's face lit up. "Look at you, old man, kickin' it with the ladies. I thought sources were off limits."

Jim felt his face grow hot, seconds away from full tomato. "Fuck you," he shot back. "It's to help her cope with the heroin cravings. She was half dead and covered in vomit when I found her in a trailer off Route 4. Hell, if it wasn't for her shacking up with a fugitive she would be dead." *And look where you are now. Right back to square one.*

"What happened to the boyfriend?"

"He's in a bag at the morgue. Greedy bastard gave himself a second dose after doing Sherri. OD'd right on the spot." Jim pinched the bridge of his nose. He'd already said too much, but felt a burning desire to defend his relationship with Sherri—a gut-wrenching need to confide in someone, even if that someone was Rob.

"Case closed."

"Maybe for us, but not for her." He was the only one to visit her in the hospital. She broke contact with her family years ago, and her "friends" had only stuck around for the drugs. "Near broke my heart seeing her like that, laying there all emaciated under the hospital lights." Jim rubbed the leaking emotion from his eyes, trying to calm his nerves. The drinks were making him babble like an idiot. "So, I've been helping her out. Pulled her in on a couple cases—you know, the little stuff, like reporting on dealers and small drug buys—giving her what little cash I can get approved." He cursed himself again for making it official. Should never have put her on the books, jeopardizing his job for something as stupid as sex.

No, it was more than that. He'd saved her, brought her back from the edge. Now she would do the same for him. He felt his chest burn at the thought. Wanted to crawl into the disgusting bed, pull the covers over his head, and cry like a baby. After all the hard work, the secrecy, the love, he'd stopped the roller coaster mid-ride and brought her here. And for what, to save his marriage? Yeah, right. Career? The more he looked at the new guys like Rob, the more he felt like a has-been. Couldn't even type with more than two fingers. Maybe it was just time to check out. He glanced at his watch again. *Any minute now.* He wasn't sure how much longer he could stand to wait.

They sat in silence for a long moment, watching Sherri take deep breaths, inching toward bending her body in half. Rob cleared his throat, causing Sherri to glance up at their shared wall. The night turned noticeably awkward.

"So...uh...who's bringing the goods?"

Jim hesitated a moment. He'd kept the identity of the seller to himself when he'd called Rob to ask for help. The squad had received a briefing earlier in the day on the newcomer, and it wasn't good.

"Plum."

Rob replayed the name in his head several times until it clicked. "Plum. J. Plum?"

Yes, J. Plum. A violent neo-Nazi turned quasi-drug dealer. Jim stared at the monitor, guilty as charged.

"What the fuck, Jim? He beat three of his 'customers' within an inch of their life and took off with their money."

"I know."

"He's going to kill her!"

I know. Jim took a deep, shaky breath. Sherri sat up on the bed, startled by Rob's sudden outburst. For the first time, the thought sunk in and felt real to him. *You're setting her up.*

"We need to call this off, Jim. This is crazy."

Jim held his head in his hands, mumbled, "Too late."

They heard the growling noise of the battered pickup truck from a block away as it closed on the motel, its muffler dangling above the asphalt. Plum swerved into the parking lot, engine alternating between sputter and rumble as he settled the truck into a spot in front of the agents' room. Jim listened to the soft tick of the cooling engine. Dug his fingers into his thighs and tried to think but the cylinders wouldn't fire.

Think!

Heard Plum hit the pavement as he jumped down from the cab and slammed the door shut.

Choose, damn it!

Heavy boots spit gravel as they stepped from the lot onto the sidewalk that lined the front of the rooms.

Now or never. NoworneveR. NowornevernoworneveR.

Jim leapt to his feet, threw the lock and ripped open the door. Plum froze, mouth wrapped around a hamburger, bag of fast food clutched in the crook of his left arm. He towered above Jim, larger than life, scarred prison tattoos crisscrossing his exposed skin. He left the burger clenched in his teeth and reached for the small of his back. Jim threw open his jacket and drew his pistol, gun barely clear of the holster as he fired. The first shot missed wide of Plum's legs, but the next three took him in the groin and midsection. Plum brought his revolver around, slinging crooked rounds in return as the pain registered on his face. Jim got off four more through the greasy bag of food before he felt his arm go numb and he lost his grip on the weapon.

Two more shots thundered from inside the motel room, spinning Plum to the ground. Rob burst from the room, kicking the dying man's gun away before glancing back at Jim, who'd slumped against the brick facade, shot twice in the shoulder. Rob stood pale-faced in shock over the fallen giant. The next moments felt like an eternity.

Sherri crashed out of the adjacent room, legs weak as she stumbled over to Jim, eyes welling with tears. She took Jim's face in both hands, kissing his mouth and cheeks and eyes and forehead, willing the pain away. Hugged him tight and whispered, "I love you," in his ear. It tickled, briefly, and sent warmth to his heart that dulled the pain in his shoulder. She smelled of spiced vanilla. He pulled her close with his good arm and closed his eyes.

When he opened them, Rob was on his cell phone, calling for backup. Jim tried to relax in Sherri's arms. Despite a few veteran tricks hidden up his sleeve, he was still going to have a hell of a time explaining this one.

Bitter Work

THEY found me in Piccolo Corner just after seven. The restaurant is long and narrow, like a boxcar, and buried in cool darkness apart from the low light hanging over the bar. I was seated near the back, finishing my meal in a booth tucked into a small private alcove. The booth lay in the shadow cast by a lone tea light flicking in a small glass jar. A serrated steak knife rested glistening over a pile of gristle in the center of the plate. I was supposed to meet Candy, but she didn't show. She was like that sometimes, and since I wasn't a paying customer I tended to understand.

We had met at Piccolo twice before, Candy and I. She liked the place, said it was romantic and that it reminded her of the dark alleyway restaurants in Italy. I didn't think a dame like her ever made it out of Chicago, but she had some rich clients whose pastimes included private planes and public displays of wealth. I gave her the benefit of the doubt on most things when I'd sit drunk on vino, listening, staring into her eyes; eyes that glowed like a cat's in the candlelight. Candy was one of my first contracts for Luciano. Before I met her I thought she was just another one of the girls so I handed it off to Lucky. He was supposed to look out for her, but got blitzed one too many times on the job and I had to step in to save face. My jaw must have been hanging wide open when I first laid eyes on Candy, because her driver gave me a light slap on the cheek with his leather-gloved hand and told me to cut the crap. Touching the wrong woman could get a man killed in this city.

She had a look about her that chiseled a piece off a man's soul. So I contented myself by looking deep into those green eyes and reserved my hands for other fish in the sea. I'm certain my lips would have joined Lucky's on the bottle if I wasn't so busy taking care of the underbelly.

I should have known something was up when the waiter returned to take my plate. He was a new kid, young. His voice cracked as his shaking hand retrieved the remains of my meal, slowly reciting the dessert menu as if a mistake would put him out on the street. Or dead.

"I'm not feeling dessert tonight, kid, but thanks," I told him. He gave a nod and walked away. I should have kept the knife.

In the waiter's absence lurked three men carved out of black and denim, blocking my exit from the alcove. They blotted out what little light the restaurant grudgingly gave up, and when the skinny one spoke the candle flickered toward him as if he was taking the rest for himself. I don't meet people face-to-face in my business, but I could tell they knew me. My black book is filled with people who have taken a bullet to the face when confronted and their brain went haywire. Or who shot themselves trying to pull a gun out of their waistband. I like to let things play out in life.

I took a long inhale through my nose like it was my last. When they didn't get the joke I floated about the pistachio ice cream, the largest of the three squeezed into the booth next to me and I wished I'd run for it. His belly gripped the edge of the table like a mouth. He put an arm around me and toyed with my tie. The dry cleaner was going to get my suit on the way home. I placed my hands on the table—transparent spectators. The candlelight licked our faces in the gloom.

"D'ya know why we're here, Watt?" The skinny one lisped out smoke from across the table, probing for answers he already knew. My silent response was met with a flick and a blur from under the table. The switchblade stabbed through my left hand, pinning it to the table before I could blink. My obese chaperone gripped my arm and muffled my cry with a sweaty palm that reeked of diesel. It hurt like a bitch, but I was happy to still have all ten fingers.

I've made a career out of others' mistakes. Do a favor for someone in a bad place and your name gets around. Soon people start paying you and you wish for things to go to hell so you can step in after with a solution. That is, until you arrive there first.

The third man leaned back, staring into space. He was too clean-cut to be rolling with these thugs, like he had dressed for a part in the play but forgot the Vaseline and coffee grounds for the beard. Skinny pulled out a small manila envelope and upended it on the table, spilling photographs. The photos were a blur in the dim light and the throbbing of my hand, so he flipped them over one at a time and slid them in front of my face. They showed a man and a woman next to each other on a stained hotel mattress, their hands resting behind their heads, elbows pointed out awkwardly. The man was shirtless, exposing a deflated gut and thick gold chain that hung low by his armpit. The woman's dark-colored dress was torn but looked like it was fixed to cover her up before the pictures were taken. I knew it was the work of Dirty Nick.

Nick had an obsession with putting his victims in bed. He once drove two hours in rush hour traffic with a dead guy in his trunk just so he could make it look like he was jacking off under the covers in his own room. Rigor mortis had started to set in by the time he got there, so Nick settled for piling the man's collection of Playboys over his body. When Detective Bronson gave me wind of it, I should have let Nick go. But I didn't. As weird as Nick was, the drugs hadn't found him yet and he was the least of my worries at the time.

A few photos in I recognized the man, even with the bullet hole under his left eye. Dom Gorlami. He was a small time pusher from New York. Word was he had brought a considerable amount of money to town. That and he was often seen around Baltic Lounge was all I knew. I'd arranged for Nick to make the hit more than a week ago. He'd been late. Nick's drug habits had been taking a turn for the worst. I wasn't planning on working with Nick any longer.

The woman was more difficult. Her face had been beaten plum. Her lips were bloodied, nose a swollen mess. Her neck was tattooed with red lace outlining fingers. The actor pushed the last photograph forward, either trying to look tough or speed things up. I didn't know and I didn't care. He tapped it twice with his index finger as if to say, *This is the one. Now you understand?*

I understood. Candy's hollow eyes glowed in the photograph. My face flushed. My hand twitched, igniting a flare of pain. I motioned to grab the knife but the monster next to me twisted my wrist and flattened my face against the wall.

"You're getting soft, Watt." Skinny jerked out the knife. He cleaned it with the tablecloth, dabbing at it like he was cleaning crumbs from his mouth. "You're lucky we're letting you clean this up." The actor blew out the candle and they left me clutching my hand in the dark.

Candy. She wasn't mine, but I thought of her all the same.

***

I walked home. The wind was coming hard off the lake and my face burned as badly as the bloody hand I had wrapped in a napkin and stuffed in my suit pocket.

I flipped a switch by the door inside my apartment that turned on all of the lights. Candy liked to remind me that I wasted electricity. Call me paranoid; I told her it was all or nothing. I tossed my jacket over a chair and assessed my hand. My sleeve was soaked halfway to the elbow in blood. The cut was bad. I poured a double vodka from the freezer, then rifled through one of Candy's purses she'd left after work. She'd often come over after jobs for a drink and to relax. I found the pills I was looking for and choked them down with the vodka.

I placed a bowl in the sink and ran the tap until it was scalding. Gritted my teeth and buried my hand in the bowl. It felt like I was back in Piccolo, the skinny guy sawing back and forth, up and down with the knife. I stamped my foot on the linoleum and clenched the counter until it hurt with my good hand. When the pain began to subside I got a bag of peas out of the freezer to wrap my hand. After closing the door, I paused at the sight of the napkin bearing the imprint of Candy's lips. Swallowed hard. Candy had left it awhile back when she was over between clients. She'd even taken the time to add a little *xoxo* underneath the lipstick. I'd hung it on the fridge with a flamingo magnet from my trip to Miami. She joked that my apartment was her safe house if it ever went to shit.

Well, it did go to shit and I wasn't there. I threw the bag of peas at the kitchen wall and it exploded, showering green marbles in every direction. I'm good at internalizing emotions, but I was two seconds away from smashing everything in the apartment. I squeezed my left hand in a fist and the pain shot me back to reality. Some rubbing alcohol and gauze and I was as good as gold. I gloved my right hand and headed for the door.

I walked out of my apartment the same way I came in—empty-handed—plus a bandaged mitt and a decent buzz. I don't own a gun, and I'm not about to carry a Louisville Slugger across town. I'm a middleman. The less flashy and dangerous, the less chance my number comes up.

I waved down my ride. An old Checker cab with bits of rust beginning to climb out from the undercarriage.

The driver was a gray-haired black man with a voice so thick and deep I frowned, thinking it was wasted on cab chatter. I gave him an address two blocks from Nick's and we tore off into the night.

"Cold off the lake tonight," he said. I shrugged out of my suit coat and laid it like a rag across my knees. The cabby went on about the weather and how he was glad it was too cold to snow. The drawl of his voice was drowning me in a vat of jazz-infused molasses.

"GasLight's got a whiskey special tonight, if that's your thing. Nothing like a good sip of bourbon."

I shuddered, tasting vodka-infused bile in my throat, and asked him to turn up the heat. Every winter I ask myself what the hell I'm doing in this frigid city. Snow flurries streaked by and I asked myself again.

When we stopped, I gave him a tip as large as the bill and left my suit coat in the back of the cab. The more alibis the better. He said much appreciated and that his name was Earl. He fished out a business card. It said DRIVER, with the name Earl Jenkins and a phone number underneath. It was cream colored and unblemished. I wondered if it was special, for people like me. Earl gave me a nod and left in search of his next passenger. I hustled the two blocks to Nick's building, passing the Blue Bird and Timothy's, almost stopping to derail myself with drink. Or would that just push me farther over the edge? I didn't pause long enough to contemplate.

The black and white veined marble in the lobby reminded me of chess, a game I always lose. I used to pass jobs for Vincenzo Milano. He was well over 70. We'd meet in Durso Park and play chess while surrounded by pigeons. I hate pigeons. The old man would always bring a loaf of stale Italian and crumble it all over the cement. The routine went on for years, until Mick and Danny Rourke threw Vincenzo off the roof of his retirement home. I hadn't met a single person I'd done work for in the five years since.

When I entered the elevator, I pressed the button for twenty-five with my thumb and watched it light up green in the dim light. One of the lights in the gilded ceiling was out and the other flickered, winking on and off as the car climbed floor after floor. I stared at my haggard face in the door's mirrored reflection. My eyes were bloodshot, sleeves rolled, shirt untucked and wrinkled. It felt like my heart had packed its bags and moved into my skull. Whatever pills I had taken from Candy's bag were not working.

A chime signaled my arrival as the doors eased open exposing a narrow hallway adorned with salmon paint and gaudy brass lighting. An irregular pattern of scratches and divots extended down the right wall as far as I could see, chips of plaster dotting the carpet. I found Nick's room at the end of the scar. Whatever had been forced into the apartment had cracked the doorframe. The door was locked but the knob was loose. I placed my ear to the door and listened. My heart was beating so loud and fast, I pressed my luck and bet it was empty, putting my shoulder into the door. It crashed open and the knob came off in my hand. So much for subtlety.

I quickly closed the door and pressed myself against the wall, letting my eyes adjust. The apartment was empty. For some odd reason, I pocketed the doorknob. The place was small. An open kitchen and den, with a bedroom off to the side. Mismatched furniture was crammed around a beat up television set. The far side of the den was glass from floor to ceiling, a giant window to the city. All that was missing was a telescope. For as dirty as Dirty Nick claimed to be, his place was fairly clean. I had a hunch it was more his methods than his lifestyle that had earned him the nickname. For a second I worried I was in the wrong apartment, until I spied the large trunk that had been dragged into a corner of the den.

It was old and beat up, a corner coated in plaster dust from the hall. The lock had been forced open and torn off. I cracked it open. The inside of the top was covered in a collage of girls and Dom Gorlami. He looked drunk in every photo. In the trunk lay thick bundles of hundred dollar bills, haphazardly over each other, as if fighting to be the first one claimed. I thumbed through one of the stacks. It smelled like a book that had been left in a public restroom. My pulse quickened and I massaged my temples. Too much money for simple drug pusher.

At a sudden noise in the hallway—a scratch on the wall like someone scrabbling for balance, followed by heavy footsteps—I froze. Adrenaline kicked in and I was moving into the kitchen, hands fumbling for a weapon, anything, my eyes focused on the outline of the door.

"What the fuck?" Nick's voice. He jiggled with the door and then pushed it in. Swayed in the light of the hall before closing the door with a thud.

When I hit Dirty Nick in the back of his fat head with the silver meat hammer from the kitchen, he had just pushed the dimmer in his living room to full. The room exploded in a blazing, hospital-quality light and I stood exposed in a high-rise apartment in the middle of Chicago, a beacon for every creeper in four blocks with a pair of binos.

The blinding light was like a camera flash in the face, causing my swing to come down in a funny angle over Nick's right ear. He crumpled in a heap but didn't go out. He just fell over onto the white leather couch with a semi-conscious look of why on his face. His left eye twitched and his skin hung slackly. I had a similar *why* look my on face. *Why did I hire you? Why this job? Why Candy?* I gripped the arm of the couch to keep myself from vomiting from the sick crunch of the mallet on his skull.

I stiffened my grip on the couch until my fingers hurt. My face felt like it had spent a month in the desert. Sweat began to stream down my scalp, the short, shaved hairs quickly losing their grip. I took two steps closer to Nick and stood over his fallen body. Dark blood was pumping out of his head into the creases in the leather. There was a soft patter as it dripped onto the wooden floor beneath forming a small puddle, prepping to advance on the nearby shag rug. There were many things I wanted to say at that moment, but I was shaking and my teeth clenched shut, refusing to obey orders to open.

Nick mouthed a few words. Maybe he was trying to apologize, maybe he was cussing me out. Probably he was just trying to breathe. I brought the hammer down again hard with the intention of finishing him off. It slipped in my sweat-soaked grip and hit Nick in the face, erasing his fat nose. Blood sprayed on my khakis. He let out a sickening moan and I threw up the vodka double all over his shirt. It was ugly.

I regained my senses and lunged to the wall slapping down the dimmer. The room looked covered in rust and the lights hummed in my ear like a fat bee. I dropped in a heap in the chair across from Nick. I don't kill people. I don't have a clean-up checklist. Hell, Nick appeared to always make it up on the fly. I pulled a toolbox over from next to the trunk. Holding Nick's metal pliers in my sweaty hand, I envisioned pulling out his teeth one by one and clipping off his fingers. My stomach turned. The whole time I couldn't take my eyes off the sheen of Nick's exposed teeth. Then he coughed up blood and I realized he was still breathing. I grabbed a pillow and pressed it over his bloodied face. Gooseflesh spread over my back and arms. He didn't struggle much.

As Nick twitched for the last time, it hit me that I really had no plan. I felt trapped and panicked and needed to get out of the apartment, away from the mess. I rummaged through his closet and donned a warm, puffy jacket. Then I returned to the trunk and stuffed as many bundles of cash as I could fit into the pockets. Buried under the cash was a .22 handgun and silencer. After some hesitation, I ditched one bundle for the silencer and stuffed the gun in my rear waistband.

I placed a call to Bronson to let him know that I was in some shit, took the elevator to three and used the walking bridge to the parking garage across the street. I could count on Bronson. He was a detective in Homicide who knew to keep some secrets and pass others. By no means was he unique, but I'd nurtured the relationship and made sure to send cash his way. Between the press and organized crime, most in CPD were getting their tickets punched.

Before I knew it, I had walked five blocks and was standing outside Parker's Tavern off Ashland. I couldn't remember my last visit so I figured it was a safe place to get out of the cold. The door jingled as I stepped inside. A couple of locals played cards over buds in the front while a lonely pool table held down the back. A stout bartender with a scraggly beard was mixing a drink for a blonde at the bar. The air tasted like a shot of vodka and a gun swirled in my mouth like a suicidal lollipop.

I took a seat three down from the lady and ordered a bourbon. I don't drink bourbon, but it was the first thing that came to mind. It didn't matter. When I caught a glimpse of the woman in the mirror behind the bar, I forgot about the entire night; the thugs, Nick, even Candy. The woman's white-blonde curls framed her pale face in a bob. Her eyes were rimmed in black, and along her jaw ran a curiously thin scar. She wore a fancy cream-colored dress, with a black shawl wrapped around her shoulders. She smiled; her cheeks were like small plums, her lips full and blood red.

"If you're going to sit and stare, you might as well come on over," she said with a wink and beckoned to me. My face flushed. I slid my glass down and took the stool beside her.

"Betty Phillips," she said. "And you are?"

"Watt Lancaster," I said, stumbling. I was struck by her forward attitude. She gasped at the site of my bandaged hand and I told her I hurt it helping a friend remodel his place. Betty said her apartment always had something wrong with it, but her landlord was a bastard who kept pushing off the job.

We seemed to hit it off pretty well. Then she asked what I do for work. When I'm asked what I do for a living, I usually tell people I crunch numbers. It's easy and boring and no one asks for details. Tonight I just stared at Betty with a mind still unable to process the past several hours.

I heard the door jingle and my eyes briefly left Betty to watch the newcomer through the mirror. He was alone and decked out in a weather-beaten leather jacket, jeans and dark boots. He didn't appear to mind the cold; probably dropped off. I felt his eyes on my back for a second too long, but I let it go.

"Betty!" called the stranger as he made a beeline for the bar. I turned slowly, watching his hands in the mirror.

"Oh, hey, Roger," she said as he almost tackled her off her stool in a bear hug. She rolled her eyes and stuck out her tongue. I could smell the stink of his breath.

"What are you doing at this fine establishment tonight?" Roger gestured toward the front door. "Shouldn't you be out on the town with Antonio?"

"He stood me up again tonight." She rotated her martini on the bar. "Anyhow, I've got Mr. Lancaster keeping me company tonight." She tilted her chin, pulling out her most darling look. I downed my bourbon, eyes locked in her gaze. She owned me.

Roger's face lit up. "Mr. Lancaster, eh? Roger Malloy." He put his hand out and I accepted his dead-fish shake. "Bourbon? Bartender, two bourbons." Roger stepped in close and saw my bandaged hand. "Let's make 'em doubles," he said with a wink, forgetting to smile.

I thanked him and then he was off to play pool in the back. The balls clattered from the break as Betty and I sat in silence. The bartender answered the telephone behind the bar and after a good chuckle, handed me the receiver. It was Bronson, quick and to the point.

"Tonight's a no go. Watch your back."

I cursed Bronson, and whoever was paying him more, under my breath and sucked on the bourbon. At least he had the courtesy to find me and give me a heads up. Betty wrinkled her brow, concerned.

"Looks like I've been stood up as well, Betty." I chuckled, trying to hide my fear, and held up my glass. "How 'bout we make a night of it?"

She beamed. We clinked glasses and downed our drinks. I told her I'd hit the john and then we'd go someplace nice. I paid and headed for the back. Roger was aiming a shot at the eight ball as I walked past. His fingers were in the game, but his eyes were on me. The guy was an amateur; I was surprised he didn't draw on me right then and shoot me in the back.

The restroom was a foul pit. A constantly flushing urinal hung next to two graffiti-ridden stalls. I turned the faucet on one of the two sinks, closed the door on the right stall and entered the left. I pulled the glove back on my right hand and assembled the .22 and silencer. It was heavier than I thought, and I checked the safety twice before carefully stepping onto the toilet lid in a crouch.

Just as my knees began to burn and my mind started screaming, *What are you doing?*, I heard a commotion outside and the door banged open. Roger stumbled in, .45 in one hand and a crying Betty in the other. His shadow moved toward the right stall. I didn't wait, crashing through the door as he was mid-kick into the other stall. I squeezed off three rounds, two of which took him in the throat. His scream came out a gurgle and painted a wide stripe on the stall door. He dropped his gun to clutch the wound. I grabbed him and shoved him back down into the stall, wedging him into the corner. He was too weak and in shock to fight back.

Betty opened her pretty mouth to scream and I cupped my hand over it. I was as shocked as she was. Her face was red from where Roger had struck her, and streaked with mascara. I pressed my forehead against hers and stared into her eyes. They glittered with uncertainty, and I wanted to kiss her and tell her everything was going to be all right. I took her by the hand and led her from the bathroom into a dark, empty bar.

We ran out through the emergency exit and into the night.

Nor'easter

RANDY felt the squelch of his tennis shoes as he stepped around the slush-drowned sidewalk in front of Doyle's Tavern. The depression near the entrance flooded with the least bit of rain, and in the winter, as soon as the salt trucks made their first run. It had been that way for decades and always would be, giving the locals something to bitch about while Tom poured their first round.

Randy clutched his hat to his chest as the wind picked up, ruffling his long white beard. The falling temperatures stung his cherry-red cheeks and nose, near matching the color of his suit.

Just one drink. Just one drink to warm up.

Forecasters had repeated their call for a Nor'easter throughout the day, promising a white Christmas after several snowless years of drab browns and roads slick with ice. It was the constant talk of mothers waiting in line at the mall. Nostalgic excitement dashed with frayed nerves at even the mention of travel plans. They kept their young ones in tow, plying them with treats to keep them occupied until a brief moment on Randy's lap. Smile, FLASH, and it was over. Off with memories in hand and

167

onto the next one. He missed years past when he could spend a moment or two with a child, get a glimpse of the innocent wonder in their eyes. Nowadays parents were too busy to wait for a conversation with Santa, too worried about what Santa might say or worse, do. And so was Corporate. One complaint and you were kicked to the curb, replaced by a fill-in forty-something-year-old administrator with a fake beard.

Randy wiped his shoes against the stone steps, slick from early customers. The broken bell above the door clanked once when he entered.

"Well look what the reindeer dragged in." Tom grabbed a remote off the bar and turned down the volume on the hockey game. Like his father before him, Tom knew every face that walked through the entrance. "Merry Christmas Eve, Randy."

"Yeah, yeah. Ho, ho, ho." Randy nodded toward the small television wedged in the corner near the ceiling. "How we doing?"

"Replay from last night. A wicked mess, but the B's pulled it out."

Though Randy loved all Boston sports, football was his game. But the Pats were having a rare difficult season and a series of losing Sundays had left him depressed and dreading the playoffs.

"Doug moving my stool again?" The stool three in from the right wobbled when he pulled it away from the bar.

"I'll tell him to knock it off."

"Tell him to fix it," Randy said, replacing the broken stool with the one on its left. His stool, the one on which he'd scrawled his name in black marker underneath the seat. "He's the one who knocked it over and gave it the limp."

"Well it's the holidays, right? Maybe I'll wake up in the morning to a brand new set."

"And Brady will run for a touchdown." The men shook hands. Randy leaned his backpack on the stool beside him and laid his cap on top. "I'll believe it when I see it."

"Keg just kicked. I'll be right back."

"You know, Tom?" Randy sucked on his front teeth, scratched the roof of his mouth with his tongue. "Hold that thought. Gimme' a coffee instead."

"Oh yeah?"

"Figure maybe it's a sign."

"You got it. Just brewed a fresh pot for myself."

Tom selected a dull ceramic mug from a mix of drying glassware, filled it to the brim and set it in front of Randy. A bit of the dark liquid sloshed over the side, slowly dripping until it paused near the bottom, lacking the weight to finish the trip. Randy wiped away the bead and licked his finger.

"Cream?"

"All set, thanks. I've had more than my fair share of sweets today." He patted his belly for good measure. "No longer a requirement for the job."

"What, Santa's Union been hit hard by that diabeetus? There goes your excuse. I'm going to remind you of that, you know."

Randy chuckled. "Baby steps. I'll make it my New Year's resolution."

Tom pulled a damp towel from his belt and wiped down a section of the bar that he'd already cleaned. It was a habit when talking to customers and not pouring drinks. The man couldn't sit still.

"Plans tonight for ol' Santa? Last minute deliveries in that bag of yours?"

"Just my boots." He patted the backpack. "Gotta keep 'em in top shape for next year."

Tom tilted his head and raised an eyebrow as if to say, *is that all?*

"What's that face for? I'm one of your best customers." He lowered his face to the mug, careful not to spill. The hot liquid seared a cracked molar on the left side of his mouth. It was past saving and should have been pulled weeks ago, but the holiday season was Randy's busiest time of year.

"You should be giving *me* a gift." He grimaced as he set the mug down.

Tom leaned over the bar and flicked a bit of pink ribbon that stuck out of Randy's backpack, exposed between the two zipper pulls.

"Taken a liking to pink then, are you?"

"Ah, that…"

Randy sighed, more ashamed than embarrassed, like he'd been caught with a stolen pack of gum and ordered to return it to the drugstore. He fiddled with the zipper, opening the bag just wide enough to pull out a small package wrapped in pink paper, its edges worn, discolored and creased. The ribbon, once curled with scissors, had since bent and flattened out in places. A corner of the package caught as he pulled it out, a small tear revealing a white box beneath. He pressed the torn wrapping paper closed as if staunching the blood from a fresh wound, and if he pressed hard enough, it would heal. His face bunched up like a child's who'd fallen, more confused at the sensation than hurt.

He took a moment to himself, cradling the present in his hands before he spoke.

"Same thing every year. It's for my granddaughter… just haven't been able to give it to her."

"What a minute now. You have a granddaughter?" Tom slapped the towel against the taps. "All these years and you never told me."

"I've never met her. You know how it is… haven't spoken with my daughter since the divorce."

"That was close to a decade ago."

"Yeah…"

Randy sat hunched, so low he could almost press his forehead against the bar. Tom played the bartender, trying to cheer him up, but Randy only listened to the muffled sounds of the television. He'd procrastinated enough, any longer and the depression would sink in. He'd switch to beer and inevitably miss the bus home. The stool rocked beside him as he slipped the present and hat into his pack.

"Well I better get going. Snow's going to hit eventually."

"Coffee's on the house. Go deliver that package, Santa."

Randy gave him a thankful nod. His shoe squeaked as he turned for the door.

The much anticipated snow storm finally began while Randy waited alone, shivering at the bus stop. The plexiglass housing blocked much of the wind but small white flurries still found their way in, dancing against

171

his face and melting on his beard.

He cursed himself for telling Tom about his granddaughter. The man played Randy's unofficial shrink, always lending an ear after a tough day. And perhaps after all these years he had a right to be upset at Randy for withholding such an important detail of his life. But some things you keep to yourself, let rattle around in your brain no matter how much it hurts.

What had it been, five years now since she was born? More? He'd never forget the day he ran into his ex-wife at the grocery store and she dropped the news like checking off an item on her to-do list. Randy had suffered through a lot in life, but nothing took his breath away like that moment. He still felt his chest tighten when he thought of it. His ex would tell him he didn't deserve their attention, that he'd passed up every chance to earn his way back into their lives after all of his poor decisions. Deep down, a sliver of Randy knew this to be true and it hurt like hell.

By the time the 42 arrived, the ground was covered in white and the snow plows were out in force. The bus was empty except for a young couple at the front. They slumped together, each propped up by the other's weight, staring out into the blizzard. The snow was so thick it resembled a fog, forcing the driver to slow to a crawl. Randy hugged his backpack against his chest for the duration of the trip, checking every few minutes to make sure the gift was still inside. What should have been a ten minute ride took close to half an hour as winter tightened her grip on the coast.

He couldn't recall the last time he'd taken the bus out to see his family, but he knew the route by heart. Still he kept watch out the window, training his eyes for street signs and landmarks to make sure he didn't miss his stop.

When he stepped off the bus the snow was up to his ankles. Close to three inches of powder on the ground and drifts twice as high against the houses. The quiet neighborhood looked like it had just received a fresh layer of frosting with glowing lights sprinkled underneath. How could it be that he was the only witness to such a scene, torn from a storybook? He took it all in, committing it to memory—the hint of pine in the air, the pale moon and its reflection upon the snow, the scent of wood fireplaces warming homes. Snowplows would arrive soon, taking it all away with sand and salt.

He threw his backpack over his shoulder and carved a path down the sidewalk toward his daughter's home. The fresh snow was quiet underfoot, puffing up around his feet, not wet enough to pack. It was a short walk, only three blocks from the bus stop, two straight and a left. His heart fluttered with each step, the full weight of the evening finally coming to bear.

Three fan-blown snowmen danced in a yard next to a series of wooden reindeer complete with sleigh. Further down the street, two giant nutcrackers guarded a front door. He smiled at the cheesy holiday cheer that never got old, even after spending a dozen holiday seasons in the mall. He could never get enough.

He slowed his pace as he turned onto his daughter's street, her house the second on the left with the large bay window. The streetlight near the driveway was out, making the house shine even brighter in the dark. The roof was rimmed with icicle lights, bushes along the front of the house wrapped with red and green strands. The blinds had been pulled aside, displaying a large, colorful Christmas tree.

His nerves got the best of him as he approached her driveway, and he grabbed hold of the base of the street light to steady his legs. Inside on the couch sat his daughter, her husband and his ex-wife. The television reflected on their glum faces. Randy slumped against the post. Had she gone to bed already?

Inside the house, the adults' heads turned, full of excitement. Not one but two little girls crashed into their parents' arms, the latter needing help onto the couch. *Two girls?* They each held a package in hand, faces beaming as they showed off their chosen gifts. Always allowed one present on Christmas Eve. A tradition he'd started with his daughter. They tore off the wrapping paper to reveal some kind of doll and tackled their grandmother with hugs and kisses. Their mother and father joined in, and soon they were in a bunch, laughing on the floor.

Randy wiped tears from his eyes. The joy inside the home crushed and melted his heart at the same time, the mix of emotions spilling down his face. This was the joy he'd been in search of, the joy he'd been missing all these years.

He couldn't intrude and risk tarnishing that perfect moment.

The younger of the two girls pressed her face to the window as he crossed the driveway, retracing his steps to the bus stop. He winked and gave her a little wave as he passed. One day, if they thought of him, this was how he'd like it to be—just a jolly old man passing through the night.

After missing two buses, 'out of service' scrolling through their displays, Randy unpacked his boots and slipped them on. It would be a long walk home, but he had all the warmth he needed to get there.

The Things We
Leave Behind

JOHN smoked half his cigarettes within minutes of setting foot inside the fall carnival. Let each stick burn down until he felt ash gray his fingertips. His hands shook as he thumbed a dull gun-metal Zippo. One piece of his old uniform he took comfort in never having to polish. He'd lost his confident stride mere yards past the entrance. Found the need to sit down on an overturned crate. The Montgomery County fairgrounds were packed with onlookers, from as far south as Louisville and as west as Indy. Could hear it in the twang, or lack of in their voice. Lou-uh-ville, not Lou-ee-ville. Private Schweitzer had corrected him in basic. John supposed Dayton was close to the South but he didn't speak a lick of it. Had trouble understanding the conversation when southern folk got together in groups larger than two. Union men from the National Cash Register factories dragged their women to have their fortunes read and get a glimpse of the Strongest Man in the Midwest, or the old-timer who could swallow a twelve-inch blade. It was all tame to John, like most things since the war. Strength didn't matter when you had a gun in your hand. Blades were bayonets that came out when things got real ugly. He used to have nightmares of those times, but now the images flickered through his mind like a silent film on repeat. Anger, fear and death all just variations of gray floating in the background. Most of the time.

"Somethin's missin' from those eyes of yours, Johnny," his father had said. Not the first words spit from his cancer-stricken mouth when John returned home from Germany, though they might as well have been. It was true that a part of John had been left behind—the softness around his midsection and the glow of a seventeen-year-old boy who lied about his age. But those were things that every soldier lost, that heal or return after a few home-cooked meals. No, what John had left behind was at home, the one thing he couldn't take with him to the front lines. The guilt he chose to carry instead rotted his heart.

He pulled his cap low as he scanned the crowds again, flicking ash into the mud at his boots. The sun began to dip, highlighting the Ferris wheel that stood guard over the right side of the field. Dark purple tents, almost black, with bits of yellow to highlight the acts, formed a row of oddities to his left. 'The Dog-faced Man', 'Lola, the Beautiful Tattooed Savage', 'Boy Quicksilver.' The rest lost to John, hidden behind long lines of thrill-seekers, eager to spend a coin for a glimpse of madness.

'Carnival Courbè' read a sign on the main tent in the center of the field. 'A Most Unusual Show, Games and Wonders.' On cue, a shirtless man spat fire into the air. Wonderment alright, he thought. How long will people fall for this charade? Like most traveling shows, the carnival had appeared overnight, announced only by a small ad in the Dayton Daily and fliers posted on Main Street.

John pulled out a copy of the ad from his pocket, wrinkled creases distorting the image. Fifth down on the bill it read, Come see the amazing boy juggler - balls, torches, pins, he does them all and more! John had no doubt in his mind who it was, the face a perfect mixture of their parents. Charlie. Still, he could barely utter his brother's name. Only seven years old when John parachuted into France. What was he now, ten? The face in the photo showed signs of a hard life, aged well beyond a teenager. John felt his insides twist, his vision gray, reliving the moment he returned home a hero.

He remembered how the dried out wood itched his fingertips as he stood on the porch and watched his father drag his heels through the dirt, back toward the house, maintaining the same worn down pace, even though John was sure they had made eye contact.

John's temper got the best of him that day and he took off, almost at a run, mud spraying over the last of his pressed pants and shined shoes. Before his father could open his mouth, John spoke the words, "Where's Charlie?" His father told him and John near beat him to death right there on the muddy road behind their house. Carried scars on his knuckles to remind him of that day when his worst nightmare came true. Later, when he'd cooled off, John helped his father into the house and gave him a bag of ice for his face. They sat across from each other in the dark for a long time, his father in his chair, John on the couch. When his father was ready, John listened to him tell the story.

Charlie had run off less than a month after John

boarded a bus full of GIs eager to fight the good fight. Or in John's case, escape from a bitter home. Charlie often hid in the woods or outback in a tent, so their father thought little of it. But those times John had been with Charlie, had been there to protect him and bring him home safe. 'Charlie would eventually come back, just like you from the war,' he said. It was no secret that their father despised Charlie, blamed him for their mother's death. She was the love of his life and granted him the only bit of order he'd ever possessed. John could hear it in his father's voice, even after the old man had been beaten senseless: Charlie was better off gone.

John had written to Charlie every month while he was away, unaware of the circumstances at home. Letters likely stacked somewhere in the house, or burned in the fireplace. John didn't want to know. It hurt too much to think about the letters going unread. Might as well have been lost at sea.

John clenched his teeth as the fire-breather reached a crescendo with two short bursts followed by an explosion that earned a few screams and burned away the fog from John's eyes. The man's mustache and eyebrows smoldered, but he bowed and went about collecting his things as if that was how the act was supposed to end. Fans dropped change in a small bucket he had set aside. John shuddered. How it could all go wrong in a blink.

Sailors on leave from Cleveland milled about discussing which attraction to head toward next, whether one more hot dog or beer was in order before hitting the bars on Brown and turning the night up a notch. Part of the crowd dispersed toward a tent containing 'Maxime The Glass Eater,' only to turn back upon hearing renewed cheers. John jumped to his feet. The fire act was only to warm up the crowd for the main event heading their way. A feeling in his fingertips said something important was about to happen. Like in the war when he'd taken cover seconds before a shell left a crater where he had once been standing.

But nothing did happen, at least for a short time. He lost hope. Perhaps he had imagined his brother's face on the flier. Night was quickly approaching and made it difficult to see, adding to his anxiety. But then he saw them, three silver orbs, shining in the twilight as they looped high in the air and then down, disappearing into the crowd. Before he could process the scene, John's legs were moving, eyes locked on the twinkling light. He didn't hear the jeers of those in his path. Didn't feel the wetness from spilled drinks as he knocked shoulders, bumping into groups on his way. He followed the act as it moved forward at a slow pace toward the center of the field. The three orbs were soon joined by a fourth and by the time it stopped moving, there were five flying high. John pushed his way through the growing circle until he reached the clearing.

A thin boy wrapped in black, white ruffles ringing his neck and hands, tossed the five spheres, faster and faster. First in a large circle, then in loops, his hands moving this way and that. The entertainer's outfit sagged on his arms like it had been soaked in water and was two sizes too big. John rubbed his eyes upon seeing the face of the boy. It was Charlie, right? It had to be. The boy's features faded in and out of focus in the gloom. His eyes were sunken shades and rough stubble was all that was left of the boy's once wild hair. For a split second the world around John became white as snow and the boy one of the many children he'd stumbled upon roaming the burnt out villages in the French countryside. Left behind, sick and malnourished, holding hands with death. The flashback punched him in the gut and he fell to his knees, clawing at his shirt. A red-headed dwarf with black lips and a torch circled the crowd, motioning with his hat to widen the circle. John could still smell the scents of burning hair and sweat left behind from the previous act. It made him gag, and he stumbled backward when the dwarf swung the torch near him. A second dwarf, dressed in matching black and white garb, stood next to the boy, two more silver orbs in his hands. Gasps from the crowd signaled their addition to the juggler's routine, now at seven.

Satisfied with the size of the circle, the black lipped dwarf buried his torch in the ground and retrieved a rusty tambourine from a suitcase full of juggling equipment. He slapped the instrument each time Charlie caught a ball, then every other time, alternating back and forth. Charlie—yes, it was Charlie, John was sure of it now— semi-danced to the noise, bending his knees and rocking his hips, still catching each ball like it was as natural as taking a breath. His hands were quick and sure—nothing like the awkward adolescent brother John remembered from the past. The crowd began to clap along with the beat of the tambourine, whooping and hollering as the orbs flew faster and faster. And then up each soared, one last time, higher than ever before, and down they came, falling quietly into an organized pile at Charlie's feet. John joined the fray, clapping like a mad man as the crowd roared with applause. Next came heavy pins in twos and threes and fours, tossed between legs and over shoulders. Each new act one-upping the previous stunt, a sight to behold. For the finale, fire was added to the mix. Charlie balanced a pin on his chin while the matching dwarf lit torch after torch, lining them up on the ground. The two assistants took turns handing Charlie the torches mid-juggle, until there were five sticks, burning bright and spinning through the air. The black lipped dwarf returned to the tambourine, whipping the crowd into a frenzy as the show reached the climax. And in a stunning finale, Charlie let the torches fall, as he had with the orbs, landing flame-side down, extinguishing as they plunged into the earth, burying the crowd in darkness. The fairgrounds shook with applause. The torches were re-lit, illuminating Charlie as he turned and bowed around the circle. The two assistants collected money in hats from a crowd that could barely contain the excitement. It was the greatest show John had ever seen.

When the commotion had died, John sat still, knees soaking up what little moisture the ground had left as Charlie piled his equipment into a beat up suitcase. First the balls, then the pins. Each arranged to fit, unlike the fire breather's haphazard exit. That was Charlie. His toys were always organized in a row beside his bed. The thought brought the first tears to John's eyes. Too much had passed, too much time lost running away. Charlie erupted into a coughing fit after finishing the pins, so hard his back arced like a cat and he leaned on a torch to prevent himself from collapse. When it was over he spit out a wad of dark cherry taffy-like phlegm. John screamed at his legs to move, to run to his brother's aid, but his muscles wouldn't respond. He looked down and discovered his hands caked with mud. He'd dug two fist sized holes during the performance, fingers aching from the filth scraped deep under his nails. Remembered he'd done this before, dug holes like this. Except the holes were larger and his fingernails ripped against the frozen soil. He closed his eyes as his ears began to hum. Concentrated on blocking out the images. The war would always be a constant companion, a reminder of lost time.

When he opened his eyes, Charlie had moved on, dragging the bag behind him across the field toward the tents. From the look of the objects tucked inside, the suitcase shouldn't have been heavy. Charlie tangled with it like it weighed over a hundred pounds, his face flush, reedy neck stretched taut.

John rubbed the clumps of dirt from his hands, dusted off what else he could on his pants and stood. Tears continued to well in his eyes. 'Charlie,' he said, barely a whisper. He repeated the name as he jogged after the juggler, his muscles tense and full of nervous energy. By the time his voice reached anything recognizable, his hands were on Charlie's shoulders, spinning him around. John pulled his brother into a tight hug and held him close. Felt bones, ribs and sharp shoulder blades through his thin shirt. The stubble covering his head felt rough and uneven like used sandpaper. Smelled of stale sweat and sickness. John's heart starved.

"What the hell man?" said Charlie, pushing back. "Get off me." Though Charlie had little strength, John let go and stood back. The brothers looked each other up and down. John's tears poured from his eyes. Couldn't remember a time when he'd cried so hard. The war, family, everything spilling out at the sight of poor Charlie. He looked like he'd been living in the gutter.

"What's happened to you, Charlie? It's me, John, your brother John." He stepped forward with arms outstretched. Charlie backed up, almost tripping, almost falling over the juggling case.

"Who the hell is this guy, Charlie?" the black lipped dwarf said. Charlie shook his head, caught in a moment between remembering and forgetting. "Who are you pal? You some queer?" John ignored him. "Huh?" he piped up again.

"Charlie, it's me, John. I'm back from the war. I've been back, been looking for you." He put a hand on Charlie's shoulder. "It's been so long. I'm so—"

John felt pressure threatening his knee. The dwarf held one of the pins in both hands. "Beat it pal, time's up. Plenty of other sights to see." John ignored him again, turning back to Charlie. The dwarf cracked him in the shin. John cursed, ripped the pin from his hands and kicked him in the chest, sending him rolling away. Charlie stared at his fallen friend. John gripped his shirt, pulled him close. "Stop this, Charlie. I know you're angry and I'm sorry. I'm sorry I left you. I'm sorry for everything." He tried to rub away the tears but they wouldn't, couldn't stop. He could barely get the words out. "I'm sorry. I had to leave. I just had to. It was the only way." He grabbed

Charlie's neck and hugged him again, whispering, "You believe me right? I'm here and I'm not leaving this time. We can be a family again."

Charlie stood limp in his arms, watching the dwarf return with muscle. "I'm afraid you've made a mistake, John." John backed up to look Charlie in the face. "You've made a mistake."

John didn't have enough time to follow Charlie's eyes over his shoulder. He was still in shock when The Strongest Man in the Midwest made an encore out of his face.

The strongman carried John over his shoulder as he would a towel after a long day of setup, pounding stakes and rigging rope. John was light work, even for muscles swollen from a night of performance. He reached for the flap of the manager's tent. Swept it aside and followed Charlie into the shadows within. The tent was easily twice the size of those containing the Oddities, even the 'Goldfish Girl's which was custom made to accommodate her tank. Between the darkness and the manager's collections it felt cramped. The strongman shrugged John off his shoulder. He hit the ground with a thud, snapping awake, hands clutching at his throbbing skull. His face stung. Hot to the touch, like shrapnel caught him before he could duck. Took a breath in through his nose and gagged on a clot that loosened coppery blood into the back of his throat. Tried to stand but the strongman grabbed the scruff of his neck and dropped a knee onto his back, crushing the air out of his lungs. John craned his neck upwards, ribs screaming at him as he struggled to breathe under the star's weight. Flailed his arms, sprawling further out, finding nothing but hard-packed earth and clumps of grass. The strongman quickly took hold of his limbs, twisting them behind John's back and re-centering his bulk.

The loss of control hurt John the most.

Lanterns hung in the corners of the tent swaying in time with the breeze outside. Cast dim light over foreign crates that took up much of the office, highlighted trinkets from travels throughout the United States and abroad. Yards of silk and jade figurines, coffee and spices from Europe and the Middle East. It smelled foreign. It smelled like war. The room dulled to the color of mud and faint memories of automatic gunfire echoed in the distance.

The sound of Charlie's hacking snapped John to attention. Charlie slumped on an unfinished wooden chair, legs splayed under his frail form. Dusky eyes blinked in slow motion, like he was close to falling asleep but chose instead to wake each time. Charlie. John couldn't find an ounce of air to fuel his voice. He grunted, pushed everything he had left into his legs, but he couldn't budge his captor.

"Please be still, sir," Courbè said, hands busy with scraps of paperwork behind his expansive desk. 'The police have been notified of the incident."

Courbè's voice pitched high, carried an air about it with French accents. John couldn't tell if it was faked or diluted from time spent away from Europe. Courbè hummed a tune, strumming stubby fingers along the desk. The carnival was close to another record-breaking week.

John recognized the rhythm but couldn't place it through the buzzing in his head. Charlie interrupted the tune with another fit. Tried to wipe blood away with his sleeve, but the white ruffles around his wrist left a smear from cheek to cheek. He smacked his lips like he was hungry. John couldn't tear his eyes from the horror, struggling again in the strongman's grip, trying to get just a single word out.

"Oh, just let the fly stand, Enzo," Courbè said. The strongman obeyed, yanking John back to his knees. He kept a palm on his shoulder for good measure.

John quickly realized Courbè stood, not sat, behind a desk. Maybe five foot tall at best. He wore a discolored button down shirt, rolled at the sleeves with black suspenders. A tall black hat, scuffed around the edges perched on top of his oily curls. Misshapen objects with twists and funny angles that seemed to blur, held down stacks of paper that ruffled when the wind kicked through the tent flap.

"Let me go. Charlie, this is madness." John spat pink. "You're coming home with me."

"And why would Charlie do that? Who are you?" Courbè asked. He looked bored, eyes flicking momentarily from his work.

"I'm John. Charlie's brother."

Courbè sighed like he'd heard it before. "I'm afraid that's not possible. All of Charlie's brothers and sisters are here," he said motioning with his arms to the festivities outside of the tent. "Charlie is at home."

"That's bullshit. You've... you've brainwashed him." Charlie began to speak but stopped to cover his mouth. "Look at him, he's sick, he needs help."

"We have a doctor attending to Charlie. I can assure you he is in the best of care."

"Charlie," John said, dripping with desperation.

Courbè cut him off with barbed French. John twitched, nerves on edge. The buzzing in his ears quit. The gray scene fractured, reformed in full color as if a curtain had been raised on the final act. The tent, ruins in a bombed out city. Crates, the charcoal remnants of a family. Charlie's family. What was Charlie doing in France? It didn't matter, he was sick, part of the resistance that had been captured by Nazi sympathizers, Courbè and Enzo. If John didn't act fast, he and Charlie would be put down. He scanned the wreckage of the house for a weapon, anything left behind. Then he saw it, the stock of a rifle that had been placed muzzle-side down in a barrel. He sprung, interrupting Courbè mid-sentence, surprising Enzo with his speed. Ripped the rifle out of the barrel, slung it high on his shoulder and leveled it at the strongman.

"Get back," he yelled, "Charlie, let's go."

Courbè laughed, slapped the desk. It was all a game to them. Paid off by the Nazis. Made rich for turning on their people, their allies. Enzo closed in on John, cutting off the exit. John pulled the trigger. Rifle clicked empty.

The ugly grin on Enzo's face grew so large, John swore it swallowed half the light in the tent. Before the strongman could flex his muscles, John had the rifle spun and swinging toward his face. Put him down with a clean shot to the ear and turned to Courbè. The Frenchman paled, clutched one of his strange objects tight to his chest.

"Don't hurt him," Charlie croaked. He stood hunched, using the chair to hold himself up. "Stop, I'm not Charlie. I'm not your brother." John's eyes flitted between the pair.

No doubt Charlie had been brainwashed by propaganda. He'd seen more than his share.

John quick-stepped to the exit and peeled back the flap, checking for the enemy, and finding none, motioned to Charlie, "Come on, let's move." Charlie turned to Courbè, his expression caught somewhere between thanks and regret. John grabbed his arm and pulled. Felt tendons stretch loose around bone. Wouldn't let the dead add his brother to their number. Charlie failed to protest through the pain.

"We don't have time for this. The city is lost; we need to move.' He pulled Charlie off the chair, put an arm around him as if he was placing a warm blanket over his shoulders.

Used the rifle to sweep aside the tent flap and stepped out into the night. Neither looked back.

John hugged his brother close. Circled the tent, hid in the shadows. Contemplated their next move, shushing Charlie's flak. Shades gathered less than a hundred yards away, stood in a bunched line outside of a bombed out church. No, not a church. Confusion rattled the synapses in John's brain. For a brief moment, the snow cleared and he was back, both feet firmly planted in the fairgrounds, staring up at the lights of the Ferris wheel, grip relaxing on the rifle. His face flushed, anxiety threatening every instinct.

Poomff, Poomff.

Ears pricked at the subdued thud of artillery thumping into the air. Muscles tensed for action. And when the series of explosions rocked the sky, fireworks booming white, John was gone.

"Take cover," he shouted, running low with Charlie across the field, diving behind the cab of a rusty truck as artillery zeroed in on their position. Wailing sirens of closing police cars signaled the air raid. He should have killed Courbè when he had the chance.

"Shit, I thought we'd pushed past this town." John leaned against the front tire of the truck, rifle gripped tight to his chest. "Who would have thought our last jump would have been into the middle of a shit storm." He shook with each explosion. Screams from the crowd sliced through him. Nothing he could do to save them. Sirens cut off as police entered the field. John stood, dared a look over the truck's engine. "I think it's over." Three cherries blinked in the distance. Charlie gripped his chest. Sniffed back salt as tears streamed down his face.

"It's going to be okay, Charlie. I'll get us out of—"

Poomff, Poomff, Poomff.

"Shit, it's still on. We've got to move."

Charlie's hands hit the dirt. Seized as the sickness squeezed his insides. Struggled to form words.

"I can't—"

"We'll hold this position, Charlie." John rubbed a loving hand over his brother's back. Felt the nubs of his spine. "Hold it as long as we damn well can." His voice calm. He placed the stock of the rifle in his gut and racked the action. Discharged a tarnished casing that disappeared into the dark. Pasted a death grin on his face. "Ready?"

Charlie sputtered to life, pushing to his knees. He grabbed hold of John's shirt with both hands. Sprayed blood as he spoke. "I can't go back, John. I just can't."

"But it's the only way out."

"No, you're mad. Listen to me, John," he cried, "It's me, Charlie. Your brother, Charlie."

John pierced Charlie's almond eyes, behind the tears, deep into the depths where his pupils turned charcoal black. Could almost see a reflection of himself. Maybe a hint of what Charlie had lost. What he'd left behind.

"No. You're not."

He stood, blinked back salt that blurred his vision.

Covered up behind the cab as the blue revolvers zeroed in. Cried out as the rifle spat invisible fire, downing nightmares as rounds ricocheted off the hood into his chest. Felt the boy pounce on him when he fell, suck warmth from his body. Felt at home watching their blood swirl. Brothers of a sort. That's all he could ever ask for.

Acknowledgements

Thank you to the writers and creators who pushed and inspired me over the past five years. These stories are the result, and I can't thank you enough. You've taught me more than you know.

Thanks to the editors and teams behind Needle: Magazine of Noir, Beat to a Pulp, Crime Factory, Plots with Guns, All Due Respect, Flash Fiction Offensive, Noir Nation, and Fox Spirit, for believing in my work and publishing many of the stories within this collection.

Thanks to Jenni, my first line editor and most important listener.

These stories (listed in no particular order) have appeared elsewhere in one form or another:

Union Man (NEEDLE: A Magazine of Noir, 2014)

Bringing in the Dead (Noir Nation No.3, 2013)

Vacation Package (Flash Fiction Offensive, 2013)

Beyond the Sea (Beat to a Pulp, 2014)

Napoleon of the North End (Plots with Guns, 2014)

Blind Spot (All Due Respect #4, 2014)

Bitter Work (Crime Factory Issue 15, 2014)

Nor'easter (Winter Animals: Stories to Benefit PROTECT. ORG, 2013)

The Things We Leave Behind (Noir Carnival, 2013)

About the author

Christopher Irvin is the author of *Burn Cards* and *Federales*, as well as short stories featured in several publications, including *Thuglit*, *Beat to a Pulp*, and *Shotgun Honey*. He lives in Boston with his wife and two sons.

CPSIA information can be obtained at www.ICGtesting.com
Printed in the USA
BVOW05s2144201115

427984BV00002B/15/P